PUNKZILLA

PUNKZILLA

ADAM RAPP

CANDLEWICK PRESS

Copyright © 2009 by Adam Rapp

First paperback edition 2010

Library of Congress Cataloging-in-Publication Data is available.

Library of Congress Catalog Card Number 2008935655

ISBN 978-0-7636-3031-7 (hardcover)
ISBN 978-0-7636-5297-5 (paperback)

10 11 12 13 14 15 BVG 10 9 8 7 6 5 4 3 2 1

Printed in Berryville, VA, U.S.A.

This book was typeset in Granjon.

Candlewick Press
99 Dover Street
Somerville, Massachusetts 02144

visit us at www.candlewick.com

For K.

March 4, 2008

Dear P,

Hey.

I'm finally writing you back. I've been carry-ing your letter around in my pocket so it's pretty wrinkled but you have good penmanship or cursive or whatever they call it so it's still totally readable. It actually looks like Mom's writing and I never knew that about you.

I've been meaning to write back for like weeks I swear P but every time I started to do it I would get distracted like I'd have some shit to do or I couldn't find a pen or something. I've never been much of a writer anyway even though this one time in seventh grade I was in detention for skipping class and I had to do this five hundred word essay on politeness and after she read my essay the woman who was running detention this substitute teacher everyone called Mrs. Boobjob told me I had an unusual gift. She wound up giving my essay to this English teacher Mr. Douglas-Roberts and he invited me into a special composition class but I got kicked out right away for chirping like a bird during this thing called an automatic writing exercise. I haven't really written anything for a while so I hope this letter doesn't suck too bad.

So I'm on a Greyhound bus and the driver's wearing a hockey mask. It's clear instead of white and you can see his skin all slimy and pressed up against the mask. When I got on he said hello and his voice was clogged and small. I think he has some sort of infection on his face and I can't tell if he's black or Mexican.

I'm wearing this hoodie I found the other day and I wish I had something a little warmer. Man I feel like shit. I have the chills and I should've eaten something but I'll have to wait for the next refueling point which the driver said would be somewhere in Idaho.

P I've been living in Portland for five months and I'm not sure how I feel about it. I probably won't really know for years because that's how it works right? You don't really develop feelings about a place till you've left it. It's like a girl or a dog like that black Lab E brought home after his pony league game that dog Sarge. Remember how Mom accidentally backed over him with the Olds and how you said he made that squealing sound? I miss that dog even though he only lived with us for a summer. Remember how you used to do that trick where you would put extra-crunchy peanut butter on the sprinkler in the front yard and he would start licking the peanut butter off and then you would turn on the sprinkler and he wouldn't stop even though the water was shooting everywhere and he would flip his weird spotted tongue around all crazy and then you would do the fake Fifty Cent voice and it would be like Sarge was really busting rhymes or something.

To be honest I've never really had a girlfriend to miss. I've gotten off here and there but I'm basically talking about hand jobs. I don't mean to be weird P but in your letter you said how you wanted the truth about stuff even if it's ugly and trust me it's going to get a little ugly. Uglier than my skittery penmanship if skittery is even a word.

I can still feel the effects of the meth that me and this kid Branson did last night. It was my first time trying it and it made everything taste aluminum so I didn't feel like eating anything and now I'm totally fucking starving but I already said that right? To be honest P I'm so nervous I can practically feel my bones rattling around under my skin.

The bus smells pretty bad like mold and breath and piss from the bathroom and disinfectant they used to try to cover it up and the back of the seat in front of me has a sticker on it that says jobops.com which is somehow making the smells worse. Out my window the sky is so dark it's almost brown like a bunch of German shepherds got stuck up there. I imagine them snarling and baring their yellow teeth at this shit world and all of its disappointments. That's pretty much all I can see the sickly sky and rain streaking slantways across the glass and the Rose Garden shrinking in the distance like a lost toy.

There are only about eight people on board and six of them look like they're sleeping with their eyes open. This man three seats in front of me is snoring so loud it sounds like he's drowning in a birdbath and this old black woman keeps crying into an Easter basket. I don't even know when Easter is. Maybe she just likes carrying around Easter baskets. She probably had something in it that she lost like some money or a picture of her dead pet. She's wearing a pink shower cap with little yellow daisies on it and she's sitting about four rows in front of me and her crying almost sounds like Santa Claus laughter. Even though it's March I keep thinking she's going to turn around and scream "Merry Christmas foolish-ass bitches!" like she's been saving up all her sorrow and hatred and this skanky bus is the only place she can let it out.

Man I wish I had that iPod Fat Larkin gave me. I wound up giving it to Branson. He's the guy I did meth with last night. He was my best friend in Portland and the one I will miss the most.

I stole about fifty iPods for Fat Larkin. Me and this kid Bobby Job were Fat Larkin's iPod thieves. Bobby Job has emotional problems and likes to stick mechanical pencils in cats' anuses especially this one cat called Acrocat who sounded like a dental drill when it meowed. The emaciated thing followed Bobby Job around with pure loyalty because he would feed it Popeye's. Bobby Job wound up getting his face bit up by a Doberman pinscher and got sent to the Yakima juvy home up in Washington.

Fat Larkin had iPod thieves and cell phone thieves and there was this girl who would stop by the Roxy Diner and deliver his daily blueberry smoothie. Oh man P you would LOVE the Roxy Diner! They got all these movie posters up like from Quentin Tarantino films and the ones Robert De Niro starred in when he was skinny like Taxi Driver and Mean Streets and the place is infested with drag queens and drug addicts and no one really gives a shit. It's your kind of place I swear.

I apologize if my writing is hard to read but writing on a Greyhound isn't too easy and by the way I just reread some of what I wrote and I realize I'm not following the rules like I should you know like grammar and punctuation and commas. I hope that's cool.

Fat Larkin kicking me back an iPod probably made him feel less guilty about Bobby Job getting his face bit up. You would like Fat Larkin P. He speaks his mind and maybe killed a few people and one of them was probably his ex-wife Norca but nobody really knows for sure. He's sort of scary-looking because he has some gold teeth and his one eye gets stuck but he has this other side like he's into Star Wars action figures and he's nonabusive to little kids and he doesn't eat pork.

He would give me twenty bucks for every iPod. I would jump joggers in Forest Park which is this big woodland preserve with all these trails and tons of trees. I mostly went for mom types or fat people because they were the easiest to knock unconscious. I'm still small for my age. I haven't grown much since the last time you saw me which was four years ago at

Christmas I think. That's when you came out of the closet and the Major made you stay at the Holiday Inn. I'm a little taller but barely five four and really skinny like you could maybe stick a pin through me or throw me off the roof of a building pretty easy. I think something's wrong with my hormones P. I wouldn't be surprised if I'm missing a gland. Maybe all that homegrown I smoked back in Cincinnati has permanently damaged me? That's what I get for smoking weed right? The point is that when I was thieving I had to target the extra weak or the super slow.

It's weird I don't feel so ashamed about confessing all this stuff to you P. Does that make me a sociopath? I heard once how if you have no shame for your bad deeds that it means you're insane. Maybe my heart has an infection in it or something or maybe when I was a baby I had some weird fever that killed part of my conscience?

After a few weeks I had to stop hitting Forest Park because these cops started riding around the trails on mountain bikes.

My iPod victims never even saw me because I would sneak up behind them and hit them in the back of the head with this heavy alarm clock that I took when I ran away from Buckner. It was my roommate Torris's clock and he got it from the cadet store. It's metal with the Buckner Military Academy seal on it and mad sharp edges so a good thump would put down even the most obese person pretty easy.

Once I knocked out this tall woman with huge veiny hands and when I was disconnecting her iPod I saw she was wearing a medical chain around her neck that said she was a diabetic. I felt bad but I don't think she died or anything because they would have put it in the paper. I have the clock in my duffel bag on the rack above me. It doesn't actually work anymore because I ruined it thieving for Fat Larkin but it makes me feel safe.

You never know what's out there P like all the murderers and the rapists and the kidnappers and the freaks who have sex with animals or children or both or the weirdos who ride around naked on farm equipment. There's just so much you have to be careful of. Fat Larkin said he was going to give me this French Taser gun that he got off the Internet but he never did. Fat Larkin has a wooden broadsword on the wall above his sofa and he can imitate fighting sequences from this kung fu movie called The Five Deadly Venoms. Once he let me hold the sword and it was way heavier than it looked. Even though he's never studied martial arts Fat Larkin says he has "world class equivalence." You would have definitely liked him P. He doesn't believe Jesus was white and he says he was Egyptian or Russian or that he was from Honduras or something.

I got another wave of iPods off these skinny girls who'd hang out at the Hollywood Bowl on Halsey Street. Most of them were like thirteen and trying to look older with their rap video makeup and tight jeans. Basically all they do is run back and forth across the lanes and text-message each other and take cell phone pictures of the local black dudes and they try talking like they know about C-Rayz Walz and Madlib and lowriders and oxycotton. The truth is they're mostly just little rich skeezers from Lake Oswego and Orenco Station and most of them haven't even had their first period yet and they get so drunk on vodka and Gatorades that they wind up puking in the ashtrays and they'd forget about their purses which I would take into the bathroom and help myself to their iPods or nanos or iPhones and leave through the custodial exit like I was never there.

I hit the Hollywood Bowl every Saturday night

for a while but then the management started post-ing signs warning bowlers to keep an eye on their personal shit so someone obviously complained. On average I'd usually get three or four iPods per visit and I got seven that third week plus an iPhone.

Fat Larkin cleans them with furniture polish and clears the hard drive and then sells them for a hun-dred cash in the back booth of the Roxy. He keeps the iPhones for himself but gives you an extra five bucks if you bring him one. The iPod he gave me has eighty gigs and a color video screen and here's the good part. There was a ton of mad slamming punk rock loaded on that iPod like Dropkick Murphys and the Dead Kennedys and the Clash and Minor Threat. P I know a lot of that scene happened way before I was born but I still relate to it thanks to your rock-n-roll teach-ings. Somehow Fat Larkin knew about my musical taste probably because I was always talking about punk rock. He even started calling me Punkzilla which everyone in Portland called me too.

Speaking of Portland the weather sucked there P. It was never sunny for more than two days in a row. Recently it's been nothing but heavy rain and this ugly brown sky so it was probably as good a time as any to leave. "Break north during a nefarious rain kid" Branson kept saying. "Break north and don't look back." North would've meant Washington State and there's nothing up there but wild animals and rivers and naked people fucking in the woods but I know north means anywhere to Branson. He could be on his way to Mexico and if you asked him where he was going he would say he was breaking north.

Branson was my roommate at Washington House and I don't think he had any idea what nefarious meant but what he would do was he would see a big vocabulary word in a magazine or a newspaper and try it out on me like I was his illiterate guinea pig or something. One time he told me that my hair looked Byzantine. This happened when we were sitting in front of Our Lady of Fatima on Garden Home Road displaying our April Yon Collection sign and trying to look legit. My Buckner hair had just started to grow out and it was getting wavy so I thought Byzantine meant curly or something.

Later that night I looked up Byzantine in the Washington House Commons Room dictionary and it said something about the Byzantine Empire so then I looked up Byzantine Empire and it said something about the Roman Empire and all I could imagine was a bunch of people walking around in togas and feeding grapes to each other and having ancient-style orgasms.

Me and Branson made most of our money from the April Yon Collection. April Yon was this little girl who got kidnapped in a bookstore and her picture was on the front page of the Oregonian and it was seriously big news because her father owns like half of downtown Portland. That guy's name is Caldwell Yon and he looks all grave and bloodless like he sleeps in a coffin and a lot of people thought maybe he kidnapped his own daughter or like sold her to this motorcycle gang who made kiddie porn but there was no evidence. He went on TV all the time and cried and looked like a vampire.

April Yon was only like six years old and the newspaper said someone kidnapped her while her mom was buying a cookbook. In the newspaper picture April has big blue eyes and pink barrettes in her hair. She's the kind of kid who you can never imagine dirty. Her skin probably cleans itself like one of those ovens.

Me and Branson made a sign with that Oregonian photo and sat in front of Our Lady of Fatima for like eight Sundays in a row and I'd ring this little brass bell and Branson would shout "APRIL YON COLLECTION! GIVE WHAT YOU CAN!

HELP FIND APRIL YON!" and we'd fake cry and all these Catholics would give us mad quarters. I'm sure Mom would have been one of the generous ones but the Major would have probably walked right by us the stingy ass.

Once this man in an electric wheelchair donated twelve bucks and patted Branson on the shoulder and told him the Lord would be proud of us. He was like "The Lord Our God would be proud of you boys" and wheeled away with his skinny dead legs.

Shit I'm suddenly realizing at this very moment how upset Mom would be if she knew about this stuff. I can just see that sad face she makes when she's about to cry. I'm sure she's really messed up about me just disappearing. I guess I would be too if I had a fuckup kid like me P. I mean I know I have ADD and I know I smoke maybe too much pot and I know I got busted stealing that DVD player in the back of the Service Merchandise and I know the Major hates me and I know all of this makes me like public enemy number one and that I totally deserved to get sent to Buckner. I know that and I can live with that but it hurts deep to think that Mom might be suffering over me it really does P. It makes me want to smash one of my fingers with that alarm clock.

Anyway back to the April Yon Collection. Me

and Branson made around thirty bucks every Sunday. Once we made fifty-seven and after we paid our Washington House rent which was twenty-four fifty we went and got hand jobs from Buck Tooth Jenny. Buck Tooth Jenny's real name is Jennifer Norris but everyone calls her Buck Tooth Jenny because she has the buckest teeth I have ever seen. But she has curly black hair and big brown eyes and nice creamy skin and she doesn't have no sores on her mouth or nothing and she looks right at you when she does you.

One time she made me come so hard I shouted "I'M A CRIME THRILLA AND A DIRTY COP KILLA!" I swear I shouted that P and even though when I come nothing shoots out I still get all those feelings in my body like I'm getting electrocuted and tickled with a feather and I'm falling backwards all at the same time.

Buck Tooth Jenny has a nice body too which makes up for her teeth and she'll sometimes take her shirt off so you can stare at her titties while she does you and shit listen to this she told us she was going to pose naked for this website lostgirlslovelosers.com but Branson freaked out on her because he's obviously in love. She was going to make like three hundred bucks posing for that website too and it's pretty funny because Branson doesn't mind if she gives me or someone else a hand job but he goes ballistic if she starts talking about posing for a website or if you call her Buck Tooth Jenny. He's like "Her name is Jenny!" and I'll say "But her teeth are so fucking buck B!" and he'll go "Don't say that shit Punkzilla!"

Once she showed us this scar on the side of her leg where she got cut going down a slide. She let me touch it for free and when I ran my finger across it she made a faraway face and it felt like a melted crayon. If she got her teeth fixed she'd be slamming but she doesn't have the money. She barely pays her Washington House rent with this disability check she gets every month for falling into a big pool of spinach where she was working at this frozen vegetable plant. She lives on the third floor and everything is mad purple in her room like for instance the walls and the carpet and even the shower curtain in her bathroom and she has all these weird baby doll heads on this shelf sort of lined up next to each other and there aren't any books just baby doll heads and some of them don't have hair and look like spooky old men.

Once after she did me I asked her what they were supposed to be and she said they were her special friends and when she started telling me their names and the little stories about each of them I knew there was something seriously off in her brain like she didn't get the right vitamins as a kid or maybe she got dropped on her head. She calls this black baby doll head Chocolate Bill. She'll go "Chocolate Bill's from the African continent" and she'll say it like she's talking to a four-year-old. She told me he liked to run through the tall grass and talk to the elephants and that his favorite thing was Oreo cookies and chocolate milk and then when I looked closer I could see that there was an Oreo cookie next to his head.

Sometimes Buck Tooth Jenny does this thing where she pretends like she's talking to someone on her cell phone. She'll hold it to her ear and say "This is Jenny . . . Uh-huh . . . Uh-huh . . . But I didn't order any cranberry plush carpeting" and then she'll hang up and shake her head like the carpet company is crazy. She's twenty-four and she doesn't have any parents and even though she's a little slow or fucked in the head or whatever she's been one of the nicest people I've met.

In your letter you asked about what I did for Christmas and what I did was me and Branson went to early Christmas Eve service at the same church where we did our April Yon thing. We basically sat in a pew way in the back and Branson pretended like he knew what he was doing like when everyone kneels and says "Amen" and all of that he was really trying to do it right. He even took communion and for some reason that made me take communion too but I didn't have to try so much because of all those times Mom made us go to St. Rose's and sing the hymns and recite all the prayers and give change when they pass those baskets around. Yeah all that church stuff is deep in my bones P. That kind of thing makes me wonder if we get hypnotized more than we know like when we're at the grocery store or at the mall or at other places where people put on nice clothes and spend money.

At Christmas Eve mass the priest was this guy with a short black beard and an oily forehead and he seemed like he was subbing for the regular priest like he had a real job selling knives or something. I'm not sure why I thought that. Maybe it was because he wasn't in a very good mood like he wasn't in the Christmas spirit. The weird thing was that when he sang his nostrils got really huge and he sounded like he was kind of whimpering with pleasure almost like something sexual was going on. I didn't like him and I hated being there and I kept trying to not stare at Jesus up on the cross because his face was really starting to freak me out and toward the end I almost left but I didn't because Branson was so mesmerized with the Catholic rituals and the sermon which I didn't even hear. Maybe he thought Jesus or Santa Claus or one of those Christian heroes with the wavy hair would grant him a wish or something?

At the end of the service this choir of little kids performed "Joy to the World" and Branson was really singing the shit out of it. It was weird how his whole personality changed like all his toughness evaporated and he was six again or something. I thought he was going to stay after and ask about trying out for the altar boys.

After church we were walking back downtown and Branson was mad silent and I asked him why he was being so quiet and he said he wasn't being quiet and I asked him if church freaked him out and he was like "Did it freak YOU out?" and I said no and he said "Stop sweatin' me Zilla" and he looked at me with animal hatred in his eyes like he was a wolf in a forest and I went "I ain't sweatin' shit" and then he said "You must wanna get blasted" and after that we didn't say anything for the rest of the walk home and it didn't snow which sucked especially after our weird conversation or argument or whatever it was. Like I told you earlier it mostly rained in Portland so there was no white Christmas but people still put up Christmas trees and you could see them all lit up in the living-room windows we were walking by. Christmas trees and angels and big cardboard snowflakes on front doors and different colored lights blinking.

When we went past this lamppost with a wreath on it Branson said "Faggit-ass Christmas" and climbed the lamppost and pulled the wreath down.

Later we went over to Buck Tooth Jenny's and Branson gave her the wreath and she hung it on the wall next to her fake tree which was only about three feet tall and smelled like a carpet store but it was okay to look at. Me and Branson decorated it with microwave popcorn and shredded newspaper and Buck Tooth Jenny arranged her baby doll heads in the branches. She put Chocolate Bill on the top like he was the Jesus angel.

Then we cooked a Tombstone pizza and got drunk on a bottle of Two-buck Chuck and sat on the purple sofa and smoked clove cigarettes and then Buck Tooth Jenny gave us hand jobs. She did me left-handed which was like someone else was doing it and I closed my eyes and imagined that girl back home who lived down the street from us Cornelia Zenkich. Remember how she would ride her skateboard by the house? I swear I could smell her sometimes P like a wild nature bush or some raspberries. I get confused by how the smell of a girl can totally haunt you. Do you ever get that way about Jorge like you can smell his cologne or his body odor even when he isn't there or like maybe when it's scientifically impossible to smell him like when he's halfway down the street or something? You probably don't even remember Cornelia Zenkich because she was like a fourth-grader when you left home. She's got blond hair and dark blue space-alien eyes. Once I caught her staring at me when I was mowing the lawn. I was mowing it with hatred for all things and I was probably making the nastiest face I could. I think you were already living in Memphis and the Major had chewed me a new one for saying fuck in front of Mom and Cornelia Zenkich was on the street in front of our house and she just stood there holding her skateboard which had all this Japanese graffiti art on the bottom of it and I stopped mowing the lawn and sort of froze and we stared at each other. She was wearing cutoff jeans and a sleeveless black T-shirt and I could feel her wanting to wave at me or tell me some secret but nothing happened.

When I was at Buckner I wrote her and asked her to come to the Midwinter Ball with me but she couldn't for a reason that makes me sick to my stomach P. So sick that I can't even go into it. Anyway sometimes I'll just think about Cornelia Zenkich riding her skateboard like her legs and her perky little ass and her titties sort of pushing up against the inside of that sleeveless black T-shirt and her soft pink nipples tasting like peppermint and then that Cornelia Zenkich smell starts making a pleasure cloud in my mind. Anyway that's what I was thinking about when Buck Tooth Jenny was giving me my left-handed Christmas hand job.

She gave Branson a hoodie with a lion on it. It said "King" on the back and Branson wore it almost every day. He even wore it to bed and to the bathroom. The hoodie started to smell and it had about nine different stains on it but Branson kept wearing it no matter what. Eventually Fat Larkin bought him a vin' Diesel T-shirt and made him give him the hoodie with the lion on it. He was like "Let it go kid. You ain't no king anyways. You ain't even a DUKE."

Buck Tooth Jenny didn't give me nothing extra for Christmas but I was satisfied with the hand job. I gave her a tin of Lake Champlain chocolates that I stole from the CVS and we ate them in about ten minutes.

I gave Branson a silver-plated cigarette lighter that this old gay guy left on a table at the Roxy. When you pushed this button it made a blue rocket flame that hissed.

"Good lookin' out dog" Branson said about the lighter. "Good lookin' Zilla."

Branson gave me a Swiss Army Knife that had scissors and all these other tools like a miniature saw and this poker thing for leather which was cool for survival but he took it back when I was sleeping and gave it to Fat Larkin who I saw using it to clean his nails a few days later.

Branson gave Buck Tooth Jenny a washcloth with her name embroidered on it and she cried. She loved it so much. You should have seen it P. Her top teeth got so extra buck I thought they were going to pop out and attack me. The washcloth was light blue with purple embroidery and I'm almost positive Branson had it made special at a department store. Now Buck Tooth Jenny uses it to dust off her baby doll heads and she sings this little spooky song to herself when she does it too. The song goes "My friends are blue my friends are green my friends are bigger than they seem" and there are other words but I can never understand what they are because her teeth get in the way.

Even though I puked from eating all that chocolate Christmas Eve didn't really suck as much as I expected it to. It was way better than the ones back in Cincinnati where everything was tense and Mom was so confused about whether or not we were going to midnight mass and before you left she was always sweating you about where you had been the night before and whether or not you were going to agitate the Major about him being a Republican war-lover and did E have one of his stress headaches and did she buy enough food and why wasn't anyone helping her in the kitchen.

The last Christmas in Cincinnati I went down to the basement and sat up against the cement wall and took like three Actifed and listened to the Dead Kennedys on your old iPod while Mom did the dishes and the Major paced around the living room preaching to E about personal excellence and achieving goals and staying physically fit. Man when I think about it I used to do a lot of Actifed. Thank god for Actifed and your iPod P. I don't think I would have made it without those two support systems.

The weird thing about Christmas Eve with Buck Tooth Jenny and Branson is that the following morning meaning Christmas morning this woman from the fifth floor burned to death and we had to evacuate the building at like nine a.m. We hung out near the lobby and saw the paramedics bring her body down on a stretcher and it was pretty eerie because the lobby was playing "Silent Night" and "Little Town of Bethlehem" and there were paramedics and firemen and this dead woman on a stretcher who had just burned to death and her face was charred like grilled chicken and they hadn't even put her in a body bag yet. I had never experienced that particular smell before P. The scent of a burnt human is unlike anything else.

She was this woman they called Black Betty even though she wasn't black. One of the firemen said she fell asleep smoking and that her hair caught on fire.

After the firemen kicked us out of the lobby me and Branson and Buck Tooth Jenny walked over to the Roxy and ate free scrambled eggs and hamburgers which was cool. I think the management at the

Roxy felt bad for everyone at Washington House. We didn't talk much but Buck Tooth Jenny kept saying she was going to quit smoking those clove cigarettes. She was obviously freaked out about Black Betty and I have to admit I was too. In fact every time I closed my eyes I could see her charred face and sometimes I still can.

P the bus is shaking too much so I'm going to stop writing now.

Love,
Your Bro

March 3, 2008

Dear Zilla,

This is a letter to wish you good luck on your bus jerny. Its been real nice getting to know you these past months, Zilla, especially at Christmas and New Years when we made bolony pizza and ate that big pineapple that Branson borrowed from the super-market. I hope you will come visit Portland again.

You are a nice boy and we will all miss you very much, specially Branson and Larkin and all our friends at Washington House. I wish I had some extra money I could give you or maybe buy a present with but I don't have any right now. I only have some checks that I have to cash. I was thinking that maybe I could give you a nice towel or some vitomens.

When you get to Memphus please write back so we know you got there with safety. I also wanted to tell you that I think you are very handsome as well as smart and that you will make some girl you'r sweet-heart someday, and you can merry her and give her sweet babies with jules for eyes and buy her chocolates and rice putting and make her very happy the same way Branson makes me feel even when he's being mean or maybe punching me in the leg or not cleaning himself. I forgive him and so does Jesus Christ and God and Santa Claws. He cries sometimes when nobody's looking, like when he's in the bathroom or hiding behind a car, and that's why I know his soul has gold in it. And your's does too, Zilla. Your's has gold and silver.

Many kisses and hugs. I hope you like my drawing of the little puppy dog. His name is Poprock and he will guard you with ferociousness.

X and O tick-tac-toe go with the flow

Love,
Jenny

March 4, 2008

Dear P,

It's a few hours later. It's dark out my window now
and I can't sleep. Man this bus is still making me nauseous like I'm not inside of it but it's inside me. I realize I sort of ended the last letter mad abruptly and
didn't really say good-bye. Sorry about that. I'll try to
be better with endings in future letters.

I should tell you a little more about Branson who
tells everyone he's from Philly. Fat Larkin thinks
he's just another stupid lost white boy from Seattle.
Fat Larkin's always like "Fool's prolly got a poster of
the Space Needle 'bove his bed. Supersonics pajamas
and shit."

I know Branson's from Waldo Ohio because I
saw his birth certificate folded up in his wallet which
I shouldn't have been snooping in but he was sleeping and his wallet was on our desk like begging to be
messed with. There wasn't any money in it just the
birth certificate.

Once when I was in Buck Tooth Jenny's bathroom I heard Branson telling her that his dad was
a professional astronaut. He was getting a hand
job and telling her how his dad had been up in the

stratosphere and how he was living on a space station and Buck Tooth Jenny believed him and went on the Internet and learned some stuff about astrology and the solar system. She started talking about the planets and how many galaxies there were and stuff like that. Another time when we were eating at McDonald's she asked Branson where he was from and he made that wolf face and told her he was from wherever she wanted him to be from and she stopped asking after that.

Branson's birth certificate says his full name is Evan Branson and that he was born in Waldo Ohio in Marion County to be exact and he doesn't have a middle name which is pretty fucked up like his parents were too distracted to come up with something. Even Mom and the Major gave us middle names even though when I say my full name out loud I feel like my mouth is full of fake dice or something. It's the name of a guy who paints the yellow lines on the highway and lives in some broken-down trailer with a lot of dead plants. I wish I had a name that rhymed like Shady Grady who was that kid who moved to our neighborhood from Columbus a few years ago. Like I said everyone pretty much called me Punkzilla in Portland.

Branson would've definitely kicked my ass if

he knew I went through his wallet. He gets in mad fights mostly with smaller dudes but once in a while he'll start something with a grown man which is really weird.

Once we were over by this big theater called the Portland Center Stage and he walked right up to this forty-year-old dude and slapped him in the face and said "What motherfucker? What?!" and the man just stood there staring at him. He was all clean-shaven and wore nice clothes and he said something like "You better walk away from me son" and then Branson got crazy and slapped him again and said "I'm not your fucking son bitch!" and the man went red in the face and just stared at him and then Branson turned and walked away and later when we were going over to the Roxy to meet up with Fat Larkin I asked him why he did that and Branson said "Punk-ass needed to be taught a lesson" and then I asked him what lesson and he was like "A life lesson son!"

When he said good-bye to me at the Greyhound station I wanted to call him his real name Evan but I didn't because I was feeling sick to my stomach and his eyes were really red and raw looking and he was drinking one of those Cokes with the vitamins in it and almost threw up after the first gulp so it wasn't such a good situation.

He told me to call him when I got to Memphis which is weird because he doesn't have a cell phone and there wasn't a phone in our room at Washington House just a payphone in the hall that hardly ever worked. I promised him I would call him but I know deep down that I may never see him again. I better go because I feel like I'm going to be sick.

I'll write more later.

Love,
Your Bro

December 12th, 2007

Dear Jamie,

Thank you for your brief letter dated December 2nd . . .

Wow, what an old-fashioned way to begin a correspondence with your own kid brother!

I was so happy and surprised, Jamie. You made my day, my week, my month, and maybe even my year, no kidding.

Yes, by the way, to answer your first question, you had the correct Memphis address. Unfortunately, Jorge and I haven't done well enough to move out of our little prefabricated, overly carpeted bunker at Stonegate Apartments. Oh, it has its charms, like the stucco walls and the false gypsum ceiling and the highly functional air-conditioning and the spleen-colored linoleum on the kitchen floor — I shouldn't complain. It just feels a bit like Jorge and I are the strange exception in some elderly community of sponge people.

And yes, we do have a Christmas tree! It's so fake it might as well be wrapped in aluminum foil, but it's thoroughly decorated and smells vaguely of chewing gum, which is better than the scent of mold, hemor-rhoidal ointment, and joint compound that seems all pervasive in our building.

So it's been a while since we've communicated. I recall speaking to you on the phone after the Major dropped the news that you would be getting shipped off to that horrible place, but after that, we lost touch, which is mostly my fault and I'm truly sorry. I've learned that being an artist is perhaps the most self-indulgent life-form on the planet; especially one who rehearses in front of a mirror seven hours a day. I rank right up there with the clown fish, who I under-stand needs nothing but occasional feeding as it has the unusual ability to self-procreate.

By the way, I promise I won't let anyone know that we've been in touch, especially our poor dear sweet mother and that military automaton that passes for her husband. You certainly don't have to worry about anything leaking from this end. As you know, I of all people in this confused, beleaguered world can sympathize with the need for a disgruntled mid-western boy to make a clean break.

So you went AWOL, huh? Now two-thirds of Wyckoff boys are official runaways! Congratula-tions on joining the club! And to pull it off at the frighteningly early age of fourteen! I was damn near twenty-three by the time I drummed up the courage! You're amazing, Jamie! I'll be the president of the Wandering Wyckoffs and you can be the secretary of state. As we both know, Edward is too afraid to run anywhere but right to where he's supposed to be, which is somewhere very near the longitudes and latitudes of his meticulously constructed master plan that lies faceup on the desk in our father's spit-shined study. Poor, cowardly, airbrushed Edward.

So at first you really had me with "P-town." I couldn't read another sentence. I had a map of the United States out and was combing every page. Is it Pittsburgh? Platteville, Wisconsin? Philadelphia? Provincetown, Massachusetts? I wondered. And then your hilarious reveal a few sentences later! Anyway, I hope "PORTLAND, OREGON, NOT PORTLAND, MAINE" is giving you a new perspective on things. I'm so glad you've made some friends. And who all is in this "Posse" of yours? Be descriptive! I want to read about these people, but most of all, I want to hear what *you're* up to, baby brother, as in where you're living, what you do at night, what you are doing to generate income, etc., etc., and spare no detail! Be frank at all costs! Gross your older, decrepit, nearing-thirty brother out!

Do you have a best friend?

Do you have a girlfriend?

I promise not to judge you, Jamie.

By the way, have you stopped smoking? If not, I hope you'll at least consider it. The stuff will not only kill the living shit out of you but will also make you broke faster than a gambling habit.

Also, regarding your AWOL status, I doubt very much that you should have anything to worry about. I can't imagine that those old potbellied, retired army men from Buckner will be spreading their big bad butterfly net very wide. It's simply farfetched to think that that contemptuous academy gives a flying piece of pornography where their boys wind up when they get away. From what I understand, with regard to tuition, it's a nonrefundable situation, so they get Major Wyckoff's carefully counted money and a simple solution to a boy's future, which is utter apathy. I can just imagine them sitting in some barracks office, staring at a map of the United States, sticking pushpins in all the cities where they think you've run off to, wreaths of cigar smoke hovering. I imagine them drinking cheap bourbon and playing Texas Hold'em, laughing themselves to sleep at the table.

As dangerous as it can be, it's probably good that

you hitchhiked and didn't leave a trail; electronic, paper, or otherwise.

So Christmas is upon us, Jamie — three weeks away to be exact — and Memphis is as lively as a slowly cooked roast. What are your plans for this festive, terrible day? I don't think there's a season that depresses me more. Last night I performed a benefit reading of my one-man show, "The Second Guesser," and the little basement theater was full. Over seventy people showed up and we charged forty dollars and I think it went over very well. It's a fairly obnoxious anti-Bush, antiwar, anti-just-about-everything piece that takes place in a small-town, southern Indiana Laundromat where two elderly ladies discover a suitcase of unmarked thousand-dollar bills, a logarithmic code that will launch a missile at any target they wish, and a special cell phone that is a direct line to the Oval Office. I, of course, played both ladies (Ethel and Doris) with grace, humor, and excellent midwestern accents, as well as George Junior (as a three-year-old). I was preaching to the choir, no doubt, as the audience was made up mostly of queers, transvestites, poets, and three or four poor wheelchair-bound souls, though one of them was rather strikingly handsome in a kind of John-Stamos-kind-of-way (that's *so not* your generation, I know). So there were no converts, but lots of laughs and a good time had by all. Jorge and I are using the money to help the theater buy a new soundboard. For all intents and purposes it was a big success and we reached our measly little goal of two thousand dollars.

So I must confess that I do worry about you, Jamie (oh, I sound just like our mother, don't I? All I need to add is your middle name, as in I do worry about you, Jamie Emmet . . .). Yes, your gay, punk, rather florid brother thirteen years your senior worries like a little granny about you. The last time I saw you — four Christmases ago, I think it was — you seemed like you were in a bad place. I'm not talking about the pot-smoking and I'm not talking about that DVD player that you stole from the loading dock behind the Service Merchandise. That's just stuff we do, and sometimes that sort of behavior, if witnessed by others — particularly the Cincinnati Police — will land you in a reformatory. I'm glad the Major, as ineffectual as the right-wing Bush fanatic is, knew that particular officer and was able to talk them out of pressing charges. And I'll even admit that as much as I hate the idea of a military school bearing down on any young man's life, I'm sure there were valuable things you were able to take from your brief time there; even if it was the simple dose of fear that might possibly act as a vaccine in your enormous, sky's-the-limit future. I'm not saying that I ever expect you to toe the line or anything as insubstantial and conformist as that; I hope that you will do quite the opposite and question *everything*—teachers, coaches, priests, lawmakers, prime-time television shows, magazine ads, top-forty deejays, and any intellectual analgesic that could numb the senses and lure you into rote compliance like it has done to the vast, flimsy-minded flock of sheep that is America.

Okay, enough sermonizing, but one more important question: What do you want to do with your life? Have you thought about that at all? Do you have any goals or things you want to accomplish? Please, please, please share this with me, Jamie. And it doesn't have to be impressive. If you want to be a truck driver, that's fine with me. You could be a stock boy in the back of a shoe store in some mall in Nebraska. As long as you're doing something that you like. Nothing would make me happier.

Okay, so here's the serious part.

I need to share some news with you, Jamie, and this is not easy. About three months ago I collapsed in the middle of the night while I was on my way to the bathroom and a few days later I woke up in the hospital to discover that a malignant tumor that was attached to one of my adrenal glands decided to explode and seed itself throughout my hips and abdomen. I lost a tremendous, almost impossible amount of blood, received a transfusion the size of Lake Erie, and I was lucky to live through the trauma. Well, I lived through that mess, but after a series of tests it was discovered that there was still a serious amount of metastasizing cancerous cells to deal with. Who would've thought, right? I mean, there isn't a soul on either side of our family that has had cancer, so call me a pioneer.

I was advised by my oncologist to receive chemotherapy treatments right away, which I did, but unfortunately it didn't work very well and the bad stuff has recently spread to my lungs and throat and I have fallen into serious decline.

Jamie, as you know I turned twenty-seven last month, and I had this sudden realization that I'm not going to make it to my thirtieth birthday. Hell, the truth is, it's doubtful that I'll make it through the next few months—I'll be lucky to get through the spring. I've grown so weak that I'm having trouble writing this letter. Jorge has urged me to tell you this news and I have resisted for a long time, partly because I didn't want to burden you, but also because the coward in me wasn't prepared to completely face up to it.

As you know, aside from a great deal of tragic sympathy I feel for our poor mother, I do not feel much of a connection to our parents. You and Edward were there at the dinner table when I tried to come out to everyone four years ago — God almighty you were a precocious ten-year-old! You no doubt felt their cold, judgmental stares as potently as I did. One can go get a good healthy injection of Novocain from their family dentist and feel about the same sensation of chilly, bloodless diffidence.

Aside from you, Edward, and Grandma Beauty (bless her sweet heart; she still sends me chocolates on Valentine's Day), I have no other family — at least anyone I feel connected to — not even Aunt Julie, who is technically my godmother. She has expressed outward disgust at my lifestyle and when she finds out about my medical state (yes, Jorge is planning on telling Mom and the Major as well at some point), she will no doubt be prouder and more confirmed than ever that homosexuality is a god-less, damnable existence. I can just see the fire and brimstone shooting from Aunt Julie's nostrils after she hears of my demise. Even though I know Edward would like to think that he is open-minded, he is so thoroughly following in our father's footsteps that I wouldn't be surprised if they wind up with the same trick knees and arthritic hips.

So, urged by Jorge, who has fearlessly stood by me as my body has started to rot and wither, I am reaching out to you, Jamie. If it is at all possible, I would love it if you could come out to Memphis and spend a little time with me before I make my merry way out of this godforsaken world. Although I don't have much money (the medical bills are unbelievable, even with the help of my Actors Equity health insurance), Jorge, who has actually sold a few paintings in the past month (he thanks you for asking!), has been kind enough to enclose two hundred dollars to help you get here. I think taking a Greyhound bus might just do it. The Greyhound bus system may be the last affordable way of crossing this inflation-riddled country of ours.

There's plenty of room for you in our apartment. The hospice people have just turned the guest room into the place where I will eventually "expire," but the study where I used to write has a daybed in it and you'll be comfortable in there.

Please give me a call and let me know if this is a possibility. The number is written in red marker on the inside of the envelope. I would love to spend some time with you before the inevitable.

Do come if you can, Jamie.

Love,
Peter

P.S. Yes, Jorge indeed keeps shaving his head, though I miss his curly hair, and Carlos is still alive and well, though he seems terribly bored by our lives as of late and spends a lot of time licking his paws, chasing an invisible, rather ingenious mouse, and staring out at nothing in particular.

P.P.S. I'm enclosing a Xerox copy of your letter because, though it is brief, I was so impressed with your writing. Read it and you'll see! And you're one hell of a speller, too.

March 5, 2008

Dear P,

I'm sorry I had to stop writing yesterday. I was mad nauseous I really was. I didn't puke but I kept feeling like I was going to. They turned all the lights off on the bus and I fell asleep and woke up with my face pressed against my window and I still have the chills but I do feel a little better and not so speedy. The sun's starting to get pretty bright and there are more people on the bus. This one guy keeps turning around really fast and holding on to his hat like he thinks someone's trying to steal it. His eyes are pretty wild so I think I'm going to have to watch him.

I had a dream about Torris Stone who was my roommate at Buckner. He's the one I stole the alarm clock from. In my dream Torris kept taking his arm off and putting it back on like not getting the fit right like it was something he bought at the hardware store that he had to return. I started to help him with needle and thread when I woke up. The bus window was really cold on my face and now my neck is killing me and I feel like the highway is some permanent movie I'm being forced to watch.

Torris Stone was from Orlando Florida and he was the blackest kid I've ever seen and the strongest too. He had an identical twin brother named Terrace and when they'd talk on the phone Torris would call him Twin. He'd say "What's up Twin you straight?" and "You got them pens I sent you?" He didn't care that there was a bunch of new cadets waiting in line for the phone. Torris liked to send Terrace pens and spiral notebooks and all this other cadet store stuff that had the Buckner crest on it. He did a lot of smiling and whispering during those phone calls too and I have to be honest P him and Terrace seemed more like boyfriends than brothers and I mean gay like you and Jorge or maybe like Elton John and George Michael.

Torris could do more push-ups than anyone in Alpha Company and he always prayed before he fell asleep and he prayed before meals too and when I asked him why he prayed so much he said it was because someday he wanted to live in a nice house with a swimming pool and have a Sony flat-screen TV. Once right before taps I asked him if he really thought praying was going to get him a house and a pool and a flat-screen TV and he said "Ain't nothin' else gonna get me that." Everyone in Alpha Company thought he was crazy.

But I left Buckner and all those military freaks running the place. They weren't going to give me my stripes before Christmas break anyway. The way it works is that all New Boys are supposed to get their stripes at the end of the first semester but I knew I was doomed to be a Recruit all year Yes-sirring and No-sirring and trying to force myself to kiss everyone's ass. I sucked bad at the military stuff P like REAL bad especially at rifle drill. There's this thing called Fifteen Count Manual Arms that involves fifteen different moves with this huge-ass World War I Winchester rifle and I could only do about seven of the moves right because it was so heavy. I was always lagging behind my squad too and we got dropped for push-ups a lot and I mean A LOT a lot like at every formation practically mostly because I couldn't keep up so I didn't make too many friends in my squad or my platoon OR my company.

Torris Stone was the only one who had any sympathy for me. He helped me practice those other eight rifle moves in our room. We used half of a broom handle that we weighted down with a metal rod and a bunch of duct tape. Eventually I caught up with my platoon thanks to Torris but I did enough push-ups at that place to last a lifetime.

Mom wrote me like four letters the first month I was there and I would write her back saying how good things were but I mostly lied and I think deep down she probably knew that. I stopped writing her back after like two letters and I think she started to panic because I got a pretty mean letter from the Major which sort of freaked me out.

In addition to me being a fuckup at drill I wasn't so great at knowing all the traditions like for instance this saying that was carved into the side of a World War II tank that was parked at the end of the Old Boy Memorial Guard Path. The saying was "By perseverance study and eternal desire any man can become great" and you were supposed to have it memorized by the end of your first formation. It's from General George S. Patton Junior and we had to know basically everything about that guy's life like all the battles he fought and what armies he commanded and this famous prayer he invented called "General George S. Patton Junior's Prayer" which goes "Almighty and most merciful Father we humbly beseech Thee of Thy great goodness to restrain these immoderate rains with which we have had to contend. Grant us fair weather for Battle. Graciously hearken to us as soldiers who call Thee that armed with Thy power we may advance from victory to victory and crush the oppression and wickedness of our enemies and establish Thy justice among men and nations. Amen."

I can say the prayer forwards and backwards no shit P and that part about the immoderate rains makes me grind my teeth because at Buckner whenever an Old Boy or a faculty member or one of the retired TAC officers would quiz me on it I would say IMMEDIATE rains instead of IMMODERATE rains and I'd have to drop and do push-ups.

At Buckner there was this Pakistani kid Abdus who they called Bin Laden even though he was fat and could barely do ten push-ups and he was mad short too like five feet two even shorter than me and the real Osama Bin Laden is supposedly like seven feet tall and has anorexia.

Abdus had an English accent he was from this part of London called Shepherds Bush and at the end of the first quarter he was awarded the Head Star for posting the highest grade point average in the corps of cadets which is pretty impressive for a New Boy considering all the pressure you're under those first few months. But the Old Boys from Delta Company were jealous and one night they broke three of his ribs when he was sleeping. What they did was they put one of his cricket balls in a pillowcase and beat him. They never got busted either because Abdus's roommate who was this Internet porn addict from Baltimore named Kenny Kandinski claimed that he slept through the whole thing. When I left Buckner Abdus was still there walking around in a flak jacket and sort of muttering Muslim prayers to himself.

P I fucking hated that place with all the old stone buildings and these portraits of the ex academy presidents staring back at you when you walked through the rotunda in the HQ. Torris was about the only nice person there. I hope he's doing okay. The faculty was always trying to get in his head because he's stronger than everybody but he wouldn't try out for the football team. They would say "Why don't you USE those muscles Cadet Stone?" and he would smile and go "Sir I DO sir. I do all them PUSH-UPS every day."

You know Buckner is in Missouri right? Man talk about boredom. Picture a cornfield and a road next to it and a car going down the road with a family in it and maybe a little kid with popsicle stains on his face staring out the back window. That's Missouri. There's lots of fields and strip malls and trees and churches and telephone poles and birds. Ohio is pretty boring and I know you know that more than anyone but Missouri is cursed with a different kind of boredom P. It hangs in the air like somebody's bad breath. People get old there and I mean like into their NINETIES.

I left Buckner in the middle of the night. At one point, I got a ride from this guy heading to Canada. His name was Carson Block and he owned a logging company in Vancouver. He picked me up in western Kansas and drove me all the way to Portland. He ate green Tic Tacs and listened to country-western music CDs nonstop which was some painful listening. He didn't have no Clash or Ramones. He wouldn't have had any punk in a million years.

Before I gave Branson my iPod there were these two bands called Liars and Deerhoof that I couldn't stop listening to. Have you heard of them P? They aren't punk bands really just alternative ones but they have some punk in them. I like those two bands a lot. There's also this guy called Daniel Johnston who is a schizophrenic and wrote all these songs in his brother's garage with Fisher-Price instruments. His songs are pretty sad and weird. There's this one called "Walking the Cow" about him walking a cow. I played it for Branson once and now he thinks I communicate with the dead. Branson said "That crazy nigga sounds like he dead. Like he a mummy" and I was like "He's not a mummy he's from West Virginia" which was true and then Branson told me I seemed like one of those people who have a thing with the dead and that's exactly how he put it. I said "What kind of thing?" but he couldn't really explain himself. We never talked about that again but maybe he's right maybe I'm meant for the dead more than for the living? Do you think it's possible that some people are on one side or the other even if they're scientifically alive? Like swimmers or nonswimmers? Even though I'm in the world and I eat and sleep like everyone else maybe the world doesn't really know I'm here but the dead know I'm here they like SEE me the way dogs can see squirrels in trees. Maybe I'm like that. I'm probably not making sense at all.

In your letter you asked me what I want to do with my life which is a mad serious question P the kind of question that makes you want to lie down and take a nap. I could be in the middle of a busy street and get asked that and I'd fall asleep because of the pressure.

When I was really little I used to think I wanted to be in the army like the Major but all that ended when I saw him freak out this one time when he was doing his morning workout. I was like seven and he didn't know I could see him because I was coming up from the basement and the door was cracked and he was doing push-ups in the living room and in between sets he stared at himself in that mirror next to the bookshelf that Grandma Beauty gave Mom and he pointed at his reflection and said "You're a warrior Major! A goddamn glory-filled warrior!" and then he kissed his right bicep. It almost made me vomit I swear P. In fact my stomach is turning right now just thinking about it! That's when I promised myself I would stay away from the army for the rest of my life but of course I went ahead and got my stupid ass sent to Buckner. How's that for luck? Don't take me to go to the casino with you no way. You'll lose all your money.

One thing I know for sure is that someday I'm going to learn how to play the guitar and maybe start my own punk band. There will be like four of us and we'll be really skinny and pale and thrash around with kitchen-cleanser hair and we'll have some crazy drummer with skin infections and jet fuel breath and leopard eyes and we'll have a seven-foot-tall bassist with safety pins in his face and we won't even have lyrics. We'll just shout a lot and play with daggers in our teeth like legit daggers with legit blades and we'll cut our tongues and our mouths will fill with blood and we'll scare the shit out of people and change the face of music in like a NEW old way. I definitely want to get a tattoo too. Maybe like a shark on my back. Sharks are cool because they never sleep and they're so invincible with mystery.

Regarding my future all I know is that I'm not going back to Cincinnati. I'm not going back to that house with the fake front lawn and the three ceramic does huddling near the mailbox and Mom's Japanese serenity garden in the backyard with its bamboo walls and blue Indonesian stones. I know that garden helps her but it makes me sad and tense when I think about her always sneaking around back there just to get away from the Major so she can just sit in peace or like put her hand on a tree because that's the best she gets.

Remember that time when the Major punished her because she hadn't been going to Bally Fitness? How he told her she had sausage thighs? How he pointed to her legs and was like "Sausages Deb.

They're turning into godforsaken sausages" and then how Mom got really still and started staring off and how she wouldn't blink even after you said "Mom blink. Please blink!" and how the Major told her he was putting her on the clock how he pulled out his digital stopwatch and told her if she didn't stop pouting in three hundred seconds he was going to go spend the night at the Officer's Club and how she stopped not blinking in exactly ninety-seven seconds and how we all knew it was exactly ninety-seven because the Major was counting them out in his command voice and how later that night we heard her crying in her Japanese serenity garden? How she waited till the Major went for his nightly drive in the Olds? And how you went out there and talked to her and sat next to her on the bamboo bench and took her hand and how she put her head on your shoulder and kept crying? What I always wanted to know was what you said to her P. Sometimes I think she wishes she married you instead of the Major even though I know that's both scientifically and religiously impossible. Plus you're gay. You would have been better to her that's for sure.

I thought it sucked how she started going to Bally Fitness the next morning and wound up losing seventeen pounds in less than two weeks. I mean I was glad that she got back into shape or became more fit or whatever but part of me wished she would've gotten fatter just to spite that fucker. Like what if she started eating mad doughnuts every morning and maybe some waffles with ice cream and gained fifty pounds just to piss him off? Remember how he was posting her weight on the refrigerator? That's some psycho control freak army-type shit P.

Before I got sent to Buckner I found a thing of Wellbutrin in Mom's underwear drawer. I Googled Wellbutrin on Edward's laptop and it said it's a depression pill. It seems like everyone's on drugs now like every American alive. There were so many guys at Buckner who had ADD like me and others who had depression and this one kid even had a problem where he would mutilate his ear till it bled. The meds line at the infirmary was almost as long as the Friday allowance line. It has to make you wonder about how long you can go without getting some kind of a prescription P. Sometimes I worry that I'll prick my finger and antifreeze will ooze out. Antifreeze or like Clorox or something. I have to admit that I stopped taking my Ritalin back in November because I only had a few extras from the Buckner infirmary. At first going off it made me feel really hyper and scattered but after a few weeks I think I got back to normal whatever normal is. I still feel like putting my head through a window every once in a while like all the way through so the jagged pieces tear my neck apart but enough of that insanity right?

Man my stomach is making crazy noises. I'm finally starting to feel like the meth is leaving my system. The last thing I ate was a cheeseburger at the Roxy for my going away party. Fat Larkin paid for it which was cool. He even put his arm around me and told me he was going to miss me. Buck Tooth Jenny showed up wearing some sort of dress that looked like a shower curtain and she hugged me like fifty times.

Don't worry P I don't plan on doing any more meth because it makes your hair fall out and puts sores in your mouth. . . .

You asked me about going AWOL so I guess I should tell you about that.

I went AWOL on the last Friday in October which was the Friday before Parents Weekend. It was my first time and I really couldn't risk getting caught based on how things were going for me at Buckner. I would have probably gotten kicked out and who knows WHAT the Major would have done to me then.

Mom the Major and E were on their way down from Cincinnati and I know they were disappointed with me because the guidance counselor Master Sergeant Mastaglio called Mom and told her how I had failed a biology vocab test and blew off a pop quiz on the first fifty pages of Of Mice and Men and got two demerits at a command reveille for the shitty job I did shining my low-quarters and how my ratings in Monday drill sucked and how my cadet morale was generally shitty. As a New Boy you can get between one and five stars at Monday drill and you have to get at least three stars for three consecutive weeks to qualify for your stripes at semester. My best Monday drill rating was two stars and I only got that once. I was the last New Boy in Echo Company who hadn't gotten three and there were twelve of us so they started calling me Dumbest of the Dozen.

At breakfast formation this tall skinny pale racist fucker from Cicero Illinois David Voyce would yell "Dumbest of the Dozen what's four plus four?" Voyce was my squad leader and hated me so much I think he got off on it like maybe he jerked off at night about how much he could humiliate me. There weren't any black guys in my platoon to harass because Torris Stone was in second platoon so I became Voyce's whipping boy. Apparently there's this place in Cicero called Marquette Park that has all these crazy race riots. Like thousands of hockey fans get together and scream "Out with the niggers!" and stuff like that. I overheard Voyce on the Old Boy phone one day asking someone how things in the park were going. It was creepy P.

When Voyce would ask me what four plus four was I would have to answer "Sir Cadet Dumbest of the Dozen reports that four plus four equals eight sir!" and then he would yell "Then drop and give me eight Dummy!" and I'd have to drop and snap off eight push-ups.

And the failure only gets uglier from there because I quit the junior varsity cross-country team too. One day we had to do fartlicks which is this exercise where you run a long road of telephone poles and you have to sprint between every other pole. After the fourth fartlick I had to stop and go to a knee on the side of the road probably because I had been smoking a lot in my room and I had burned out my endurance. The junior varsity coach stood over me and jogged in place while screaming at the top of his lungs that I had a vagina. "Vadge!" he screamed "Nothing but vadge!" and then he ran off and joined the others. I was tempted to go AWOL right then and there no shit P but I had nothing but a pair of shorts and my cross-country T-shirt and my running shoes so I turned around and headed back to campus. What's weird is I still have the running shoes. In fact they're the only pair of shoes I own. They're New Balance and they're so beat-up I had to fix one of the bottoms with Elmer's glue and duct tape.

I wound up getting three hours of Guard Path for not reporting back to HQ with the JV cross-country team plus I got kicked off the team. That same night I had a dream about Jesus of Nazareth. We were hanging out on this porch swing behind a 7-Eleven and smoking blunts and he was showing me some athlete's foot fungus between his toes. "It's blue" Jesus of Nazareth kept saying in his miracle voice. "It's blue see there?" And then this other thing happened that I don't understand which is he removed his ANKLE and gave it to me and asked me if he could have mine like he wanted to trade so we did we totally traded ankles and I felt like I became like some all-American Catholic hero all of the sudden.

P I was nervous about the Major coming to Buckner I won't lie. I knew he was going to wear his dress greens with all his ribbons and medals and those weird patent leather tuxedo shoes that weren't even military issued and he was going to strut around with his hands behind his back while all the cadets and TAC officers saluted him and kissed his ass.

A few days before I left home he knocked on my door and stood in the entrance to my room and just stared at me. I was listening to your iPod so I had to remove my earbud things. His shoulders were all sloped and I could barely make out his face because the light from the hall was on and he was mad shadowy. I thought he was going to bust me for smoking weed earlier that day or for forgetting to take the trash out or something but when I asked him what was wrong he said "You know anything about this Viagra stuff everyone's talking about?" He was trying to be all quiet and secretive. I said I didn't know anything about it. He said "Okay then" and went down the hall. I could hear him walking around the house for the rest of the night like he was taking a hike or something. I couldn't sleep because I was pretty freaked out and I could just imagine Mom in their bedroom staring up at the ceiling or trying to read one of her romance novels like reading the same sentence over and over again and just laying there frozen like a cat in the middle of the street.

There was this kid at Buckner named Tim Tiptree who was selling black market Viagra to cadets. He would sell them to Old Boys for fifty bucks a hit and to New Boys for a hundred. His dad was a pharmacist in Philadelphia so he had easy access and most of the cadets were rich so he made tons of money. If you were an Old Boy and you couldn't get off campus and find a townie girl to split one with the thing to do was to get a New Boy to stand in front of your room while you jerked off. Have you ever split a Viagra with Jorge? I hear it makes sex way more intense like you feel like you grow fangs.

By the way I don't mean to change the subject so fast but when mom finds out about you being so sick she might send you some money or at least some care packages so that'll be cool. That Christmas Eve when you came out of the closet she was the only one who didn't totally freak out. I remember how she took your hand at the dinner table and how the Major told her not to comfort you but she kept squeezing your hand anyway. I thought the Major was going to kill you that night I swear I really thought that P. I couldn't even sleep because I had this terrible feeling that he was going to sneak into your room and snap your neck.

So anyway AWOL wasn't even hard. You hear all these stories about cadets getting chased and Tasered and knocked in the back of the head with these huge flashlights that the on-duty guards carry.

What's weird is that there isn't even a fence around the Buckner campus. Sometimes during Monday drill I would be marching with my platoon and I would get this feeling that I could just march away and start running but I couldn't do it.

That Friday night the TAC officer on duty was this old Vietnam vet called Sergeant Swift and he was sleeping in the HQ and I walked right past him and across the rotunda with all those paintings of the famous generals staring at me and then I was through the front doors of DeRosa Hall and I was walking under the Academy Archway and I just kept going down Cemetery Road till this townie picked me up in a Dodge Dart. He had long hair and he was a chronic insomniac. His name was Steve and he said he worked at an all-night doughnut shop just to pass the time. He knew I was a Buckner cadet because of my haircut and he also knew I was AWOL but he helped me anyway. I had heard how townies could be pretty hateful so I was lucky.

The first thing he asked me was if they beat me at

Buckner. He was like "They beat you at that school?" and I told him that sometimes they did and then he asked if I hit them back and I lied and said yes and looked at my fist like there was a piece of glass in it.

Steve the insomniac doughnut maker drove me all the way to Pittsburg Kansas where I spent the night under this bell tower thing on the campus of Pittsburg State University. I pretty much froze my ass off and woke up face-to-face with a squirrel whose eyes were black and jittery.

That day I managed to eat for free in their cafeteria. What I did was I found this math book in a garbage can and sat down at a table and pretended like I was reading it. A few minutes later this pale girl with little baby teeth sat down across from me and asked me if I was the provost's son. I had no idea what the provost was but I was like an actor P I really was. I was totally playing it cool. She was wearing this huge orange and red sweatshirt that said "Go Gorillas" on the front. Eventually I told her that yes I was his son and I thought I had her fooled but she smiled all conceited and said "Dr. Yarworth is a she."

I said "Oh" because I couldn't say much else. When you get caught lying I've learned that Oh is about the safest response. Then she asked me if I was actually reading the math book and she was still smiling at me with her weird little teeth. I said I was and then she said she was impressed because it was an advanced calc book so I flipped a page and made a face like knowledge is boring. Then she asked me my name and I gave her yours.

She said "Like the Rabbit?" and I went "Exactly" and then she started scratching her skinny pale arms.

I asked her her name and she said it was Margaret so I told her Margaret was a pretty name and she said thank you and got all quiet and bashful and started looking down at her lap. She had a lot of peach fuzz on her cheeks and I wondered if her hormones were messed up like maybe she burped a lot or could grow a circus beard. Then she told me how all her friends called her Mags and I tried imagining her friends and they were all pale and skinny and wore sweatshirts with gorillas on them. She told me how she was studying to be a special-ed teacher which made me remember this special-ed cadet at Buckner Floyd Bausheck who had a face like a catfish and always walked around with his mouth open because he was so congested. I told Mags she seemed like she would be a good teacher and she must have liked that because she stopped scratching her arms and offered me the rest of her chili. While I was eating it I could feel her staring at me but not like in a sexual way. It was more like I had survived a car crash.

Then out of nowhere she asked me if I was a premature baby. She said "Were you a premature baby?" and then she told me how premature babies grow up to be near-perfect human specimens. That's what she said P near-perfect human specimens I shit you not!

She told me I had a lovely face and that I possessed an androgynous beauty and how I must be appealing to both sexes. What a weird thing to say to someone right? I felt like stabbing her with her fork like I got mad homicidal feelings because of her comment. There was this huge clock in the cafeteria and I felt like it was watching me too like it knew my thoughts like it was somehow connected to Buckner and would let them know about any sudden movements I might make.

When I finished her chili I asked her if I could borrow five bucks and I told her I was good for it but she gave it to me and said I didn't have to pay her back. I think that as a general rule lonely people give other lonely people money a lot.

Later I walked into town which was pretty small

and boring with an Ace Hardware and a bowling alley and some fast-food places and a RadioShack. I eventually found Highway 69 where this guy Alan Skymer picked me up. It started raining pretty hard which helped because I looked good and pathetic when he pulled over in his Crown Victoria. Alan Skymer had a brown beard and was dressed like a janitor meaning he wore one of those navy blue uniforms. I asked him if he was in the custodial profession and he shook his head and said he was a meter man. I asked him what that was and he said "I read peoples' meters." I said "Like gas meters?" and he was like "Gas electricity water distance time . . ."

I stopped asking questions after that because every time he spoke he smiled this private smile and he would laugh in this weird way like he was casting some ancient spell that was going to give him pleasure later. He had these big yellow teeth that made me feel a little nauseous P. And things did eventually get weird that night when he asked me to put my Buckner gym shorts on. We stopped at a Motel 6 way on the west side of Missouri like near the border in this town called Joplin and when we checked in to the motel the man at the front desk asked Alan Skymer if I was his son and Alan Skymer said "Nephew" and patted me on the head and I played along and called him "Uncle."

Anyway when we got settled in our room I went to the bathroom and when I came out he had gone into my bag and laid all my stuff out on the end of one of the beds. He said "Are those your gym clothes?" I nodded and then he stared at them for a long time like he wanted to try them on or something. I kept having this feeling that the TV was going to suddenly turn itself on to some blaring talk show with like Oprah or Montel Williams or Jerry Springer. I kept waiting for that to happen but it didn't.

Then Alan Skymer asked me if he could hold my hand and I said "Like HOLD hold it?" and he said he only wanted to hold it for a few minutes. He had mad bad breath P like beef stew gone bad and KFC coleslaw but I let him do it anyway.

His hand was big and hairy. Up close he had one of those faces that seems young and old at the same time like a shop teacher or some guy who owns a store where you take broken-down kitchen appliances. Maybe his brown beard had something to do with it. He looked at me really intense-like for a minute and then his face turned all red and he closed his eyes and put his head in my lap.

So I can't believe I'm telling you this P but then Alan Skymer said "Can I get closer?" There was something in his eyes that I trusted. I'm not sure what it was because like I said before he had been laughing in that weird way and he had those big yellow teeth but I nodded anyways. He had those sad pleading eyes that clowns sometimes have. Clowns and Saint Bernards.

I had never gotten a blow job before P but I just closed my eyes and tried to imagine Cornelia Zenkich from back home like her walking around naked on our lawn and then leaning back against our maple tree and that really helped a lot. When I came he said "Isn't there anything?" and I said no that I didn't come like that yet and he seemed a little disappointed.

When it was over Alan Skymer kept telling me how beautiful I was and he asked if he could do it again but I said no and he was very polite and good-natured and then I told him I was going to go sleep in the car because I was feeling mad disgusted and I kept looking at myself in the motel room mirror and sort of hating what I was seeing like my eyes and my mouth and the way my nose sort of turns up a little at the end like a fucking rabbit and he said "Okay

okay" and then I put the things back into my gym bag and went out to the Crown Victoria and tried to lie in the backseat and not think about what had happened. There were cars parking and leaving and people talking and headlights panning across the windshield and it made me feel really lonely and unsure of things.

About an hour later he came out to the car and watched me through the rear windshield. I rolled the window down and he said "I just wanted to say good night." He was wearing wire-rim glasses now. He went from looking like a shop teacher to looking like some nerdy freak librarian. I said "Okay" and then he said "Good night Neph" and went back into the motel room and turned the light off.

"Neph" made me really anxious and I started clawing at myself like at my chest and neck and I was clawing so hard I thought I was going to make myself bleed. I eventually stopped when the red streaks started showing up on my face. I could see them in the rearview mirror. I looked like I had run through the forest and gotten scraped by a bunch of low-hanging tree branches.

I couldn't sleep but I didn't get out of the car because I thought if I did I would try and murder him. I was going to use my alarm clock but I wasn't confident that I could hit him hard enough because Alan Skymer had a pretty big head. But the next thing I knew I had my alarm clock in my HAND like I was squeezing it really hard and I was out of the car and there was the smell of diesel fuel and the sound of cars driving on the highway and then I tried to open the door to his room but it was locked and so I was going to try sneaking in through the window but then the door opened and he was standing there in a pair of pajama bottoms that had yellow smiley faces all over them and he wasn't wearing a shirt and his chest was weird and flabby and hairless and he said "What's wrong?"

I didn't know what to say and I was totally fucking busted and I looked at my hand which was holding the alarm clock and I said "I thought maybe you'd need this to wake up tomorrow" and he said "They got one next to the bed" and I said "Cool" and he said "Thanks for thinking of me though" and I said "Sure" and then I turned and walked back to the car and sat in the backseat and started squeezing the alarm clock so hard in both hands I thought I was going to break it.

We didn't talk much the next day. Being in the

car was like being trapped in a museum or something. He wouldn't even put the radio on. I didn't stay in a motel room with him that night even though he offered. It was a nicer one too with a pool and a Jacuzzi.

P I never found out much about Alan Skymer like what he meant by calling himself a meter man or why he wore the same blue janitor's uniform the next day. I did see him put this gold ring on though so I'm pretty sure he was married. What's weird is that I can't remember what kind of license plate he had and I never forget those details. It was a strange experience like strange in a scientific way but I'm glad he drove me all the way to the western edge of Kansas to this little town called Goodland. He let me out in front of a movie theater where one of the Shrek movies was playing. He said good-bye and gave me forty bucks and I used six of it to see the movie and another four for popcorn and Coke. There were all these families lining up to see the movie. Lots of little kids with Kansas Jayhawks T-shirts and baseball hats. For some reason I felt really bad for all of them. I wanted to yell at them to run away while there was still hope to like get the fuck away from their parents and board a ship to some deserted island or some place where they could create their own society with their own rules but I didn't even open my mouth. I don't remember anything about the movie because as soon as it started I fell dead asleep.

That night after the movie theater cleared out I met Carson Block who's that logger from Vancouver I was telling you about before. He was standing outside the theater next to a black SUV with Canadian plates. Some terrible country song was blasting out of the driver's side window and I was like Oh shit no not country music but I couldn't be choosy right? Carson was obese like maybe three-hundred-some pounds and he had a big meaty face and one of those extra chins and he also had a little red mustache and wore cowboy boots. After he took his shoe off and shook something out of it, he turned to leave and I asked him point-blank if I could get a ride with him. He turned and saw me and said "A ride where?" and I went "As far as I can get." Then he like sized me up a little and asked me if I was in some sort of trouble but I said no and that I missed my ride and then he asked me what direction I was heading and I said north. I have no idea why I said north P it just came out. Maybe it's because of Santa Claus and the North Pole or the North Star or some ridiculous shit like that.

He said he was definitely going north and asked me where my parents were. And I said "That's who I'm trying to get to. My parents." Then he asked me where that was and I said Oregon and I have no idea why I said that because I had never even THOUGHT about Oregon before. He said "Portland?" and I said "Yeah Portland."

The he pointed at his SUV and told me to get in.

The inside was huge and all leather and smelled like a candy apple. I was still pretty clean-cut with my Buckner hair so I'm sure he thought I was a decent enough kid and not like no punk or nothing. He didn't talk a lot but he liked to use this toothpick to stab at his gums. We listened to just about every famous country song there is. I liked the stuff by Johnny Cash the best. Carson never sang along to anything or turned up the music. I think he had some serious ice water in his veins. His stillness made me want to smoke like crazy but I didn't dare ask him for a cigarette because not only did he seem like the last person in the world who might smoke but he also probably had some DVD about lung cancer stashed in the glove compartment.

We drove all night and most of the next day. We wound up staying at a Best Western just outside of Salt Lake City.

Like I said he was really fat but not in a gross way meaning that he showered and wore deodorant and shaved and changed his socks and underwear but man did he have a lot of loose flesh like it really flopped around in waves. In addition to being clean with his hygiene he was also really detailed about folding his clothes and keeping his suitcase neat.

Nothing bad happened with Carson Block even though I kept expecting it to especially after the dick-sucking saga that went down with Alan Skymer. Saga's the correct word right P? I'm almost positive it is.

The only thing that was a little weird was that I think Carson Block was tempted to turn me in because I overheard him talking on his cell phone in the bathroom. He was telling someone how he picked this kid up who he was planning on dropping off in Portland and he was asking whoever it was on the other end if he should "make a call" meaning to the cops I'm almost positive. Then he just said "Uh-huh" a few times and flushed the toilet.

When he came out of the bathroom I was sitting in a chair by the window. He hiked his pants up around his waist and closed the bathroom door and just stood there. I asked him if he was going to call the cops and he said he thought maybe he should but that he wasn't going to and then he said he was going to go to Burger King and asked me if I wanted anything. I said I'd eat a Whopper but I said I was broke which wasn't completely true but he said he would get me one and then he left and came back a little while later with my burger and an orange Fanta. He ate a Double Whopper with cheese in the bed and I ate my regular burger at the little table by the window in about four bites and all you could hear was us swallowing and breathing.

At one point Carson Block put his Whopper with cheese down and asked me how old I was. I told him I was fourteen and he told me I looked younger. He was like "You look about twelve. Or eleven maybe."

Then he started talking about how these days most kids look older than their age. He said it was because of all the chemicals in the cows and the "hormones and whatnot."

I told him I really was fourteen and then he didn't say anything else and he watched a country-western music channel on TV and finished his Whopper with cheese and then he went into the bathroom and brushed his teeth and came back out and watched some more country videos and fell asleep with his clothes on.

I eventually fell asleep in the other bed but I watched some more videos first. One was about this blond guy walking in the desert. He comes across an island oasis with tropical fruit drinks and a live mariachi band and this hot skeezer in a turquoise bikini. The whole thing turns out to be a mirage and the singer drops to his knees and finishes the song while the sun is setting and the skeezer in the bikini turns into a prickly green cactus. After that it was like a switch got turned off in my head and I fell asleep in my clothes too. I even tied my hoodie under my chin. I'm not sure why.

Hang on I'll be right back. . . .

P check it out so the driver just pulled the bus over to the side of the road and we had to get off because some weird guy sitting near the front thought we had a gas leak. "We got a leak!" he kept turning around and pleading with everyone. He had a face like a cartoon. The bus driver made us walk like a hundred feet away while he disappeared under the bus and assessed the problem. Cars were mad zooming by us and the weird paranoid guy couldn't stand still and the sky was sort of churning like it was going to rain again and a cop even stopped to ask what was going on so it was pretty tense. The cop made me more paranoid than the weird guy. I thought he was going to come over and question everybody but he didn't he just hung near the bus driver and nodded a lot with his arms folded.

I wound up bumming a cigarette from the black woman with the pink shower cap who got on the bus in Portland. It was a Newport and I normally don't like menthols but you have to take what you can get right? Man it tasted good like way better than food way way better. But I have to tell you something weird happened with the black woman P and it's a little embarrassing and this is what it is: she thought I was a girl. I went up to her while she was packing her Newports and I asked her if I could have one and she said "You got it girl" and gave me a cigarette. Then she lit me and said "Motherfuckin' bus always jacks up my back."

Then the driver came walking toward us and lifted his hockey mask so he could yell and said everything was okay and we all ran back over to the bus because it started to rain.

Now we're back on the bus and it's raining like crazy way worse than yesterday and I have to admit that I'm afraid to look at that black woman in the shower cap. It's like she knows something about me that's not true but maybe it is true in some fucked up way and just to prove something to myself I'm tempted to walk over to her and whip my dick out and be like "Bitch who you callin' a skeezer!"

I'm going to stop writing for a minute P because I'm getting too worked up and I almost just kicked the seat in front of me. I think there's a retarded man sitting in it eating a bucket of caramel corn hang on. . . .

Okay I'm back.

And there is nobody actually sitting in front of me. That retarded dude with the bucket of caramel corn must have moved closer to the front.

I think I need to tell you more about Branson because it sort of relates to the thing that just happened outside.

So in Portland me and Branson shared a room in that place Washington House which was this low-income place for loners and street kids. There were some maniacs there too like this one guy everyone was afraid of called Fifty Watt Dave whose head was shaped like a lightbulb. He would hang out in the fourth-floor hallway with a remote-control car and drive it up to you and try and drive it over your feet and sometimes park it in front of you and talk to you like the car had a voice and say "Wanna race kid? I'm clockin' zero to sixty in four-point-four" and weird shit like that.

The way me and Branson met was he was standing around in this parking lot outside of this bar on Burnside Street called the Crystal Ballroom. He was huffing glue out of a brown paper bag and trying to call this junior-high girl called Easy Elise on a cell phone he'd just stolen. Apparently Easy Elise used to go around bragging that she's on a milk carton back in Iowa or Illinois or someplace. She was majorly into giving head to anyone especially if you drank Bombay gin. In that parking lot Branson was dialing her number and then huffing glue. He would dial and huff dial and huff. I was just sort of minding my own business near the sidewalk because that's almost exactly where Carson Block dropped me off and I was holding on to my gym bag and trying to figure out what I was going to do next.

After Easy Elise didn't answer for like the fifth time Branson threw the cell phone against a brick wall and it smashed into a thousand pieces. I was just trying to play it cool and not get too nervous when Branson asked me if I wanted to fight him. I said no and then he asked me for ten dollars but I told him I didn't have ten dollars even though I still had about thirty bucks from Alan Skymer and then Branson just stood there sort of looking at me and started smoking a Camel Red and said "Why won't you fight me you a little bitch?" I told him that I would fight him but I didn't feel like it because I was tired. Then he asked me where I was from and I told him about how I hitchhiked from Missouri and about Alan Skymer and Carson Block and what their cars were like and what sort of music they listened to and the whole time Branson kept nodding but he was look-ing towards the entrance of the Crystal Ballroom like that little junior-high girl was going to appear. He wore this old-school Chicago Cubs hat cocked to the side and these baggy jeans and low-cut black patent leather Adidas shell toes and a white puffy ski vest with a hoodie underneath.

I asked him who he was waiting for and he said "Just this little ho. She frontin' though. Skanky-ass juice-box." Then he sucked hard on his cigarette and said "How old are you?"

I told him I was fourteen. I know I probably should have lied and told him I was older but I was too tired. Then I asked him how old he was and he said he was seventeen which didn't seem right. A few months later when I saw his birth certificate I realized we were almost exactly the same age. Branson was born six days before me. In fact his birthday is the day after tomorrow and that's partly why I gave him my iPod.

He asked me if I was in school and I said no and asked him if he was and he said "Fuck no. School's for the future of America" and then he pulled out a pair of nunchucks from the small of his back. They were black with silver diamonds on the handles and he started doing figure eights and all these kung fu combinations. Then he put the chucks away and said "Let's break north" and we walked across Vista Avenue over by where all these other punks and homeboys and runaway girls were hanging out and smoking blunts and listening to music. It was lots of street kids with bad acne talking about where the cops were roaming and where they slept the night before and where they could score good meth and heroine and poppers and who had learned how to cook crank down on a hot plate with Sudafed and Benadryl and Arm and Hammer baking soda and on and on. I couldn't see where the music was coming from but it was this weird old-school trancy drum-and-bass stuff with some girl singing in the background like she was getting drugged.

This tall skinny black dude called Tron was showing everyone this scab on his dick and he was laughing about it like it was something to be proud of. He wore a fur coat and kept opening it up and dropping these fake leather pants down to his ankles and going "You see it right? Look at that shit yo!"

Branson kept asking everyone if they'd seen Easy Elise and nobody had but some kid wearing a chef's hat said he'd heard she was in the hospital because she donated blood at the blood bank and fainted but then someone else said that that wasn't Easy Elise that it was this other girl called Sky so Branson said "I'm out" and we left.

While we were waiting for a walk sign Branson told me how he had a room at Washington House and how the top bunk was open because his boy Tom-Tom just got caught selling digital cameras out of the back of a U-Haul and how Tom-Tom got sent to some juvy home in Corvallis where they put a computer chip in your arm.

So the really weird part that relates to what just happened outside with that old black woman in the shower cap is that at first Branson thought I was a girl too. No shit P even though he wanted to fight me. He said he thought I was some dykey butch chick from Eugene who was trying to act tough and I was like "You'd fight a girl?" and he said he'd fight a dyke any day of the week because of the fact that he got beat up by some deejay lesbian skeezer called Chocolate Yoda a few weeks before after he tried to steal some of her old Cypress Hill records. He said she was like six feet tall and punched harder than his father.

Me and Branson spent like four days hanging together before he found out I have a dick. It was fucked up too because I woke up in the middle of the night with him trying to go down my pants like he was intending to finger me in my sleep or something. I kicked him so hard I almost knocked his jaw off.

"I thought you was a bitch!" he cried holding his face.

He washed his hand in the sink like nine times in a row. I think he even put toothpaste on it.

P it's not like I WANT to look like I do. I wish I could grow some whiskers or have a scar over my eye. I've even thought about cutting myself I really have just like an inch-long slit over my right eye or across my cheek because that might help me look more manly or less soft or whatever.

By the way when did you start shaving? Were you my age or did you have to wait? Puberty is like mad skipping me over. I can't wait to start becoming a man P I swear. And I'm almost positive I'm not a homosexual like you and Jorge.

"You'd be a pretty bitch you really would" Branson said a few days after he tried going down my pants. He was smoking on the steps to the YWCA. "Them old west-side sweeties would love you." He was talking about this group of senior citizen perverts who hang out on the west side and play dominoes and this Korean poker game called Thirteen. "Those light-ass eyes of yours. Your silver hair." I said "It's not silver it's blond" but he was like "That shit is mad silver!"

You couldn't imagine Branson being from Waldo Ohio. He seemed like he grew up on the streets of New York City or in some gang in Chicago. I figure he just watched a lot of rap videos or visited the right websites or something.

Once I asked him what he wanted to be when he grew up. "Grow up?" he said. "I ain't never gonna grow up. I'm like one of them donkey dudes in Pinocchio."

Regarding my prettiness what's weird is that my

hair wasn't even long when I arrived in Portland. My Buckner high-and-tight had just started to grow out and Branson STILL thought I was a fucking girl. I dyed my hair black a week later. Fat Larkin's girlfriend helped me do it. Her name was Shurl and she had this little wispy mustache that she put Vaseline on. Her and Fat Larkin lived in a residential hotel around the corner from Washington House. They had this big German sheperd called Saint Ray that only had three legs.

I stole a Clairol Nice 'n Easy kit from the Walgreens and even though it stunk and Shurl almost burned my scalp it worked so now even though you can see my blond roots most of my hair is black.

Me and Branson were hanging out on the steps to the YWCA because that's where Mrs. Mitre always gave Branson a couple of bucks for carrying her bag to her car. She's this elderly skeezer who swam everyday to ease some spinal condition. Her hands shook and she walked all hunched like a troll. She started giving me a buck too just because I was there and then me and Branson would go to the Virginia Café to play video poker. The guy behind the bar liked us because we'd help him take the chairs off the tables and mop the floor.

When he plays video poker Branson always doubles down no matter what the machine deals him so we'd either win big or lose everything. I made $114 once and it paid our Washington House rent for a month. This big guy with a pink face named O'Meara takes the rent money but he never talks to you. He just stands behind this bulletproof window all day and reads hot-rod magazines.

Spanish Dave slept on our floor for a week. He was running from some girl who claimed he got her pregnant and she was supposedly hunting him with a letter from a lawyer and a digital camcorder. Spanish Dave spoke Spanish in his sleep but English during the day. When I asked him how much Spanish he knew he said "I don't know no fucking Spanish. I can like count to FOUR and shit but that's it" but he was fluent in his sleep P I swear. He's fourteen like me and Branson but he has hairy armpits and he would get people to give him a quarter to see naked pictures of his mother that he downloaded off the Internet. "That's her I swear for God" he would say. "Look at them titties kid. Nice right?"

Man my stomach feels twisted in knots. I just hope I get to Memphis okay so I can see you P. My hand is mad killing me too so I'm going to end this letter.

I just heard an announcement that we're getting close to some place in Idaho where we'll get like a half hour to walk around and get something to eat.

Maybe that lady with the shower cap will give me another cigarette if I'm nice to her? Maybe I should tell her my name is Shirley?

Love,
Jamie

P.S. I can't believe you're dying. Please don't die.

October 10, 2007

Dear Jamie,

Hi, honey. How are you? I hope well.

I haven't received a letter from you in a few weeks, and I just wanted to check in with you to see if you're okay. I spoke with Master Sergeant Mastaglio the other day, and he mentioned that schoolwise you were doing better. In fact he shared the good news that you got a B+ on your most recent history test. I was very proud of you when I heard that, Jamie. It honestly made my day. He also told me that you're still struggling a bit with your Monday drill ratings. Just remember what your father told you: Marching and maneuvering a rifle is like anything else; it just takes concentration and a little elbow grease. I hope you're still taking your medication. I know your father and I were very detailed in our request to the infirmary nurse, as was Dr. Carroll, and as you already know, she thinks that Buckner can be a very positive step for you.

Things at home are good. The fall seems to be flying by. It feels like it was the end of August just a few days ago. It's been quite chilly this week. I just pulled all of the old wool blankets out of the trunk in the basement. You know how stubborn your father is about turning the heat up.

Edward just got word that he was accepted early to the University of Chicago undergraduate premed program. Your father and I were so thrilled! And I know Edward is relieved. I think his shoulders have dropped six inches since he got the news. He even went on a date last week. He took this nice young woman from the neighborhood to go see *American Gangster,* with Denzel Washington and that Australian actor your father likes so much. Afterward they went miniature golfing and had cheesecake at that little late-night café by the library. When he came home, his head was in the clouds and he seemed pretty smitten. I think he's in love, and your father enjoys teasing him about it.

I have been spending most of my time fixing up the basement. I just had the new paneling installed, and the carpeting is going to be put in tomorrow. Your father wants to get a pool table, and we already ordered a flat-screen TV and an entertainment system. It'll be a good place for you boys to blow off steam when you're home from school.

So the main reason I'm writing, Jamie, is to let you know that your father and Edward and I are definitely coming down for Parents Weekend. We're planning on staying in town, at the Comfort Inn. We'll arrive Saturday morning, attend the Parents Welcome Brunch, walk around a bit—I know your father and Edward want to hit the golf course for a round—and then we would love to join you for the movie in the dining hall that evening. I understand they're showing *Pearl Harbor,* which has that wonderful English actress in it, Kate Beckinsale (I think your father has a crush on her!). Then we'll let you have the rest of the night to yourself and join you again for Sunday brunch and chapel and the football game. We'll probably head back to Cincinnati after that, but you'll no doubt be sick of all the doting at that point.

Maybe when your father and Edward are golfing, you and I could take a walk and just catch up one-on-one. I'd love to know what's on your mind with regard to your future. I know you hate talking about that stuff, but a gentle conversation on the subject might be good for both of us. I promise I won't push too much, scout's honor.

Anyway, we're very much looking forward to

spending some time with you, Jamie. I can't wait to
see this short haircut!

Love,
Mom

P.S. I'm enclosing a picture of Edward and
your father at the lake house. Can you believe
the size of that fish?

October 17th, 2007

Son,

Your mother informs me that you have decided to be
a cynic and not answer her letters. You should know
that she is heartbroken about your choice to discon-
tinue your correspondence. The few replies you've
written to her since heading to Buckner have given
her great joy. I hope you will consider picking up the
pen again and letting her know how you are doing.

Speaking of your progress, I have recently been
in communication with the commandant's office, and
Colonel Stoops tells me that though you have shown
some improvement on the drill field, you are still
very much behind the others. Son, I would urge you
to take the initiative and put some extra time toward
it. Colonel Stoops assured me that if you made a formal request to your first sergeant, he could arrange
procuring a rifle for you from the battalion logis-
tics officer — I believe the cadet's name is Captain
Voskul. An extra hour a day working through the
Fifteen Count Manual movements will definitely pay
dividends. I know you are more than capable of excel-
ling in this environment. The damn stuff is in your

blood and in your bones, and we all know how smart you are. Those Buckner entrance exams don't lie. So please go knock on your first sergeant's door and make an effort.

As your mother told you in her last letter, she and I and your brother Edward are going to see you in a few weeks, at Parents Weekend. I look forward to visiting with you and hearing how things are progressing.

Love,
Dad

March 7, 2008

Dear P,

Today has been the shittiest day of my life.

I'm writing to you from the backseat of a Lincoln Town Car. There's this really old lady in the front seat whose one eye keeps leaking. I don't think it's tears it's more like some liquid form of LIFE leaving her. Her hair is so white it hurts to look at and she smells like diarrhea and old flowers. This man with blond hair is driving. He has a bald spot at the top of his head and a sunburnt neck. I think his name is Dale or Dave or maybe Dan and he's one of those adults with braces. He's really quiet and maybe like forty and he's wearing a tie and a short-sleeved shirt and he drives with both hands on the wheel. They're pretty quiet people. Every once in a while the old lady sighs. She might be his mom but she could be his grandmother too. I'm just glad I'm finally out of the rain and not dead.

The shittiest day by far P even shittier than that experience with Alan Skymer in the Super 8 Motel even shittier than when Mom and the Major took me to Red Lobster to tell me they were sending me to

Buckner and I never thought things could get worse than that. I'm okay now but about ten hours ago I got jumped in the bathroom of the Greyhound station in Caldwell Idaho.

I didn't think I was going to be able to write you again for a few days because my hand got so sore from the other letters. When I make a fist it feels like there are needles in it or something but I started getting the shakes again and I figured writing you would calm me so I'm going to give it a try.

I spent about half the morning hiding behind an abandoned Mexican restaurant staring at a big-ass cornfield and getting rained on. It's been raining like a motherfucker all day and till Dale or Dave or Dan and this old lady with the leaky eye picked me up on the side of the highway I was seriously thinking about laying down on one of those yellow lines and ending it all like letting a semi blow right over me.

So anyway back at the Greyhound station in Caldwell Idaho these dudes jumped me and stole all my shit except for this notebook. I was the only one in that bathroom pissing at the middle urinal when I heard someone come in behind me. The next thing I knew a forty of Budweiser got busted over my head. It sounded like two cars crashing deep in the pulp of my brain. They got me right above my left ear and there's a huge knot there now and I have a feeling that it's going to keep swelling and I'll wind up with a serious growth on the side of my head.

I had never been knocked out like that before P like waking up and having no idea where I was or what happened. When I came to I made this weird sound like AAUAUAUUAAUAULL all high-pitched and girlish. For a second I thought I was mentally retarded or some sort of vegetable man who lost the use of his brain. I could hear this far-away ringing sound and it took me a minute to figure out that the noise was coming from inside my head. I can still hear the ringing a little now. It's sort of mixing in with the hum from the engine of this car. At first it freaked me out but ten hours later I'm finding it weirdly comforting.

They got my wallet and this turquoise belt buckle with a black bear on it that I got in Portland. My right eye is pretty swollen too and the side of my head stings like a bitch and my ear has been bleeding off and on for most of the day. I probably have a concussion so I'm trying to not fall asleep. The dude who picked me up keeps rolling the window down every few minutes because he thinks it'll keep me conscious.

I remember learning about that concussion thing in health class when I was still in school in Cincinnati and how if you fall asleep when you have a disaster to the head that you can go into some kind of coma state and never wake up.

When I got off the floor of the bathroom I couldn't walk so good and I had to go to a knee and then I got sick and puked in the sink. I spent about ten minutes picking little pieces of glass out of my ear where the bottle broke. I probably need stitches but I can't exactly snap my fingers and wind up at a hospital plus I'm basically a certified runaway and who knows where I'd end up if the Major found me. To make things worse my bus took off without me and the driver that guy with the hockey mask knew I was in the station. He said he would wait but he didn't.

In my Buckner gym bag I had around five pairs of underwear and some socks and another pair of jeans and some Listerine breath strips and that alarm clock and a Game Boy Micro 20th Anniversary Edition that Branson stole for me as a going away gift. Even though it was from Buckner I liked the gym bag because it wasn't too big and if I needed to I could use it as a pillow. I spent almost all the money you sent me on that ticket too. Remind me to never ride Greyhound again.

But the reason I'm seriously fucked is because they got my cut of the April Yon Collection which was around a hundred and sixty bucks! I'm just glad they didn't take this notebook which has everything I've written to you so far plus the letter you wrote me at the beginning of December which is tucked into the inside pocket plus a letter from the Major and a letter from Mom and a card from her and another card from Buck Tooth Jenny and a letter from Edward and a letter from Grandma Beauty and a letter from Cornelia Zenkich and this other letter to Mom that I wrote but never sent. The notebook is mad thick like one of those ones you're supposed to use for multiple subjects in school but I'm not surprised they didn't take it. You can't really get much for a spiral notebook especially with a bunch of shitty writing in it.

I felt like calling you P but I didn't want to waste what little money I have left which I had stashed in my sock which is exactly sixteen bucks. It's the change from the bus ticket. I swear I'll keep all my money in my sock from now on.

After I picked the glass out of my head I cleaned the cuts with that cheap pink squirt soap stuff and went out to the waiting area and fell asleep on a plastic chair with lots of ballpoint pen graffiti on it and had a dream of flying gorillas. I knew I wasn't supposed to fall asleep because of the concussion rule but I couldn't help it. I think my body just needed to like shut down for a little while. The last thing I remembered was that in the ballpoint pen graffiti I thought I could see the face of Abraham Lincoln like with the beard and the black top hat and everything and check this out P it made me think about how Edward used to draw him in the margins of his textbooks how he would draw him sitting in a chair mostly but how this one time he drew him dancing in the middle of an ice rink. He didn't draw skates on him he drew him wearing shoes and there were all of these kids skating all around him. It was a really detailed drawing P did you ever see it? Do you know the one I'm talking about? Seeing Abraham Lincoln's face in the middle of that ballpoint ink graffiti made me think about how Edward has always had this secret talent of drawing Abraham Lincoln but how no one really knows about it and how he keeps it hid like he's ashamed of it or something. Do you have any idea why he would be like that?

In my dream the flying gorillas didn't have

wings. They just flew with their arms extended and their fists pushed out in front of them. There were thousands of them and the sky was mad yellow and for some reason I knew that the color of the sky and all of those flying gorillas somehow meant the end of the world like as soon as they passed overhead everything would turn dark and murky before some atomic bomb would hit. I have to wonder if those gorillas have something to do with the gorilla that was on the sweatshirt of that girl Mags I spoke to at the University of Pittsburgh that skinny pale girl with the fuzzy cheeks who gave me five bucks. She had a gorilla on her sweatshirt too! It's weird how something like that can turn into other stuff in your dream. A simple memory suddenly multiplies itself by a thousand and takes over your sleeping life. I've heard that that's how acid works. You drop a few hits and suddenly cartoon people start walking up to you asking for directions to the ski lodge and shit like that.

I woke up in the waiting room of that bus station in a serious panic and it took me a minute to catch my breath and I'm really glad I didn't wind up going into some death coma although I have to admit that at least part of me is a little worried that I AM in a coma P and this is all being written from inside my head and my body is frozen and I'm just a slab of meat on a table somewhere in the middle of Idaho with drool slipping down the corners of my mouth.

Do you remember when I fell off the front porch and cracked my head open on that fake doe in the wood-chip bed? It wasn't the three ceramic deer that huddle it was the little doe off by itself the one that's next to the mailbox now. I think I was like seven or four or something and everyone freaked out because apparently my head hitting the doe made such a loud noise and that neighbor lady with the big splotch on her face thought I had cracked through some nest of bones in my head or fractured my skull or something. It was Mrs. Loomis or whatever her name was and she had that splotch on her face and she had a shiny pink nose and Mom was always talking about how she never shaved her armpits properly. Do you remember how she came over with that neck brace thing and how Mom kept trying to put it on me? This situation is easily as bad as that P maybe even worse I shit you not. If you saw me you would believe me. Anyway remember how there used to be a fake rabbit next to that fake doe and how someone stole it and Mom thought it might have been that weird mailman dude with the old-school knee brace? Well I wanted to let you know that I'M the one who stole it P. I totally stole it and kept it in this box under all of your and Edward's old report cards. It was in that General Electric box that the microwave came in and I would go down to the basement every so often with a black Sharpie and draw on the fake rabbit. I would draw like a mustache and some tiger stripes and a black eye. When I think about it now I feel sick like way sicker than I feel when I think about all the bad stuff I did this past summer all that stuff that sealed the deal for me getting sent to Buckner. It's the rabbit that makes me feel most guilty and ashamed P.

Anyway when I cracked my head open on that doe you kept spraying me with water so I wouldn't fall asleep do you remember that P? You have to remember that! I wasn't dreaming that too was I?

After I woke up in the waiting room of the bus station off to my left this old man was cleaning a fake tree. He was moving so slowly it was like he'd been poisoned. His face was yellow and dry and he had the eyes of one of the Major's trophy bass.

I asked him if he saw anyone coming out of the men's room meaning those punks who jumped me but he just looked at me. He barely even shook his head. He was so out of it he could have been sleepwalking.

My head was pounding and my mouth was dry so I used the money from my sock to buy a packet of Advil and a Coke at the gift shop and I asked the woman at the cash register the same question. She said she didn't see anyone. The cash register woman could have been Mom's long-lost sister I swear P she had the same color eyes and the same little turned up nose like the one I inherited.

I pushed the Coke and the Advil toward her and she told me I was bleeding and I nodded and she asked me if something happened to my ear and I told her I picked a scab. "It'll stop" I promised her. She made the same concerned face Mom makes like she's doing a Tide commercial twenty-four hours a day or something and the cash register woman told me I should leave scabs alone that that's how cuts get infected and I nodded and walked away.

When I returned to the waiting area this little kid with a purple-and-gold College of Idaho coat was sitting in my seat. He was like eight years old and his hair was so red it looked dyed for Halloween. It was way redder than Carson Block's mustache which was pretty red. The kid was eating a bologna and cheese sandwich and a mini can of Pringles. I sat down next to him. After a minute he stopped eating and he covered the sandwich with a napkin and put it in a plastic bag and then shoved the whole thing in a book bag that he was wearing in the front the way little kids do. Then the kid turned to me and said "Did you fight back?" He was obviously referring to my fucked-up face. I said "I didn't even see them coming" and he said "They jumped you?" I nodded and then he told me I had blood on my ear and I wiped it off with my hand. He asked me if it hurt and I said "No" but my voice sounded weird sort of like I was talking into a paper bag. Then he said "You got more blood there too." He was pointing at my neck so I wiped it and that's when I could hear the ringing in my ears and I was starting to really freak out. He gave me the napkin that was balled in his hand. I took it and pressed it to my ear and it mad stung.

Then he asked me if I lived in Caldwell and I shook my head and then he asked me where I was from and I didn't know what to say but I told him I was just in Portland and he asked me if that's in California and I told him it was in Oregon and then he said that he had cousins in California and that they lived in Sacramento and that they got season tickets to the Kings and that the Terminator's their government and I corrected him and said "Governor" and he said "I mean governor" and told me he had just seen Terminator 3: Rise of the Machines on DVD. He was like "My mom finally let me watch the whole trilogy. In number three Arnold's called Terminatrix and he goes back in time to save John Connor. I thought it was fair to middling. The first one's way better." Then he asked if I had relatives in Caldwell and I told him I was on my way to Memphis and how I just got off my bus for a second to use the bathroom and how I got jumped and how when I came out the bus was gone. He was outraged P you should've seen him. He said "The driver didn't wait?! Where's the justice?!"

He was one of those kids who looks at you so hard he practically burns a hole in your soul. We sat in silence for a second and then I asked him what was up with his coat. I said "Are you like a genius or something?" and he said no and I told him he was pretty young to be going to College of Idaho and then he told me his dad was the basketball coach there. I asked him if his dad was coming to pick him up and he said his mom was and how he was at his cousin Larry's house and how Larry lives in McCall and how they got a lithium springs and six hundred miles of national forests and how the elevation's really high there so you have to drink lots of water or you'll get constipation. Then just like that he changed the subject and said "Hey have you ever played Cold Fear?" I asked him if that was one of the Terminator movies and he said "It's on Xbox. Cold Fear introduces a new kind of horror experience in a constantly shifting environment at sea. You get to be Tom Hansen a U.S. Coast Guard crewman whose team is sent to investigate an abandoned Russian whaling ship." I said "What if you don't want to be Tom Hansen?" and he answered right away he said "You don't have a choice. It's not such a bad thing though. T.H. is pretty cool."

Then I asked him what happens and this is what the kid said. He said "As you delve deeper beneath the ship's bloodstained decks you encounter hordes of evil creatures. To survive you must eliminate your enemies and avoid traps and attain helpful information from other characters on the ship. It's a lot like Resident Evil 4 but I think it's way better."

I told him he sounded like an expert and he said "I was the best at Super Monkey Ball Deluxe but that got boring. My friend Jay is pretty much the king of

Brothers in Arms: Road to Hill 30 but games about real wars are too weird for me" and then he asked me if I was falling asleep and told me my eyes were closing. Man I really was trying to stay awake P but this kid's subject matter was mad boring. I said "Why are games about real wars weird?" and he answered "Because it's like games about real wars made the new real war happen. Like the one in the Middle East. My cousin Larry thinks it's good though because if we get drafted we'll have skills to pay the bills. But I'd rather play Resident Evil 4 any day."

Then I asked him his name and he said it was Sam and I told him my name and he said he was pleased to meet me all professional. I think he was even going to try and shake my hand but his cell phone started ringing and he unzipped the side pocket of his book bag and answered it. The ring tone was from that rap song about how many chocolate butts can fit in the backseat of the rapper's vanilla Hummer.

Into the phone Sam said "Where are you? . . . Okay . . . Just sittin' here with a friend . . . Yeah she's nice. Her hair's really black with a stripe down the middle. She just got jumped in the bathroom and her eye is pretty swollen. . . . I don't know. Hang on." Then Sam pressed the phone against his coat and said "My mom wants to know if you need to go to the hospital."

I shook my head.

"Nuh-uh" Sam told his mom. "Yeah, she seems okay. Just a little blood. I gave her a napkin. . . . Okay. Over and out."

Sam closed his cell phone and put it back in the side pocket and said his mom would be there in a few minutes and then I got up and started to walk away. He asked me where I was going but I didn't answer him I just started moving away. I felt like I was sort of floating.

He said "You're comin' back right?" but I barely nodded and kept moving away. I had no idea where I was going P I just had to get up for obvious reasons. The Advil hadn't kicked in yet and my skull felt too small for my brain. I met eyes with the woman in the gift shop again she sort of looked at me with a concerned expression and turned to help a customer.

When I walked into the women's bathroom I could feel a sick tingling in my nuts P like I was walking through some weird fog of gasoline and animal breath or something. The women's bathroom smelled different than the men's. It didn't reek of bleach and piss and stale cigarettes and diarrhea.

It was like there was less wrong with the world in the women's bathroom and it was definitely cleaner. Part of me was afraid of getting jumped again but part of me wanted to see if I could really pass as a girl.

There was nobody in there so I went straight to the mirror. Since I ran away from Buckner my hair has gotten pretty long and it's starting to get curly and it's ugly black from Shurl's dye job especially because you could see my blond roots really coming in. My eyelid was bruised and swollen and there was a scrape on my cheek and it was starting to go purple near the scrape and there was also some dried blood over my ear where I got hit with the forty. But I have to admit I look like a girl P! Even with my face all fucked up I do! I might even be a CUTE girl which sucks so bad I could tear my own skin off!

While I was washing my face the door opened and a heavy Mexican woman walked past me. She was wearing a big pink T-shirt with a picture of Jesus of Nazareth on it and underneath it it said "Jesus Is My Homeboy." Our eyes met in the mirror and she smiled at me and went into a stall and shut the door. So it worked! I totally passed as a girl in the women's bathroom! Man that really fucks my head up P first Branson and then that black woman from the Greyhound and the little kid talking to his mother and the Mexican woman in the pink Jesus of Nazareth shirt! Maybe I need to start taking some hormone pills or something?! I don't want people to think I'm a fucking girl P! I mean I LIKE girls like in a SEXUAL way but I don't want to BE one! Does this make me like PART LESBIAN or something? Because I LIKE girls AND I LOOK LIKE ONE? These are mad confusing things for me to think about as I write to you from the backseat of this Lincoln P very fucking confusing to say the least.

When I came back out to the waiting area Sam was playing Snake on his cell phone and he told me that he called his mom back when I was in the bathroom and that she said she would give me a ride somewhere. I told him that that was cool because anywhere seemed better than that bus station. For all I know those guys who jumped me are back there right now getting ready to whack some other victim.

Then Sam offered his bologna and cheese sandwich and I took it and then he gave me an Ocean Spray cranapple juice box too. He was a nice kid P he really was. Some kids are mean but Sam wasn't one of them. If there are two forces in the world like

Fat Larkin thinks then Sam is definitely on the Luke Skywalker side.

His mom got there about five minutes later and I was still pretty dazed from everything especially the girl thing and for a second I thought I was dreaming and the subject of the dream was that I had gotten a sex change but then I remembered the flying gorilla dream and I knew it was impossible to have a dream within a dream like that but maybe it's not impossible P. Maybe this whole day has been a dream and I'm really on that Greyhound bus still like way closer to Memphis than I think. Hang on a minute I need to get to the bottom of this. . . .

So I just slapped myself in the face really really hard and I'm definitely not dreaming P. That old lady with the leaky eye turned around and asked me if I was okay but I could hardly hear her voice. It was like she had a fur ball in her throat or something. Then the guy driving Dan or Dave or Dale said "She asked if you're okay" and I said I was fine. That old woman has these little broken blood vessels all over her face like she belly flopped off the high dive or something. That leaky eye is smaller than the other one and I wonder if it's fake or if something's rotting in there.

The slap might have made my concussion worse but just to be triple sure I'm not dreaming I just cut my arm with a bottle cap that was in one of the side ashtrays. It was sort of rusty too so now I'll probably get diabetes or something. It doesn't hurt much in comparison to the forty of Budweiser but there's a good amount of blood that I'll have to keep off of their nice backseat. At least now I know for sure that I'm in the world of the living. And man it's still mad pouring rain out there and rain is a very real thing. I've never seen it come down so hard in my life.

Anyway as I was telling you just before I slapped and cut myself that that kid's mom picked us up at the Greyhound station in Caldwell Idaho. She had blond hair and a really nice ass but her face was sort of busted though because she had this big bump on her nose that looked like some sort of mini-tumor or something like if you picked at it some bugs would come squirming out but she smelled like cinnamon chewing gum and she really did have a nice bon-bon as Branson would say. I have to confess that I spent the first hour fantasizing about messing around with her.

A few minutes after she started driving it started hailing but we were in a Lexus so I felt pretty safe despite the fact that my teeth were suddenly starting to chatter on their own. The hail was pretty loud on the roof of the Lexus and Sam was like "Soon it will be raining fire" and his mom went "Sammy where do you get these things?" and Sam said "On the Internet" and then his mom said "Oh you do not either" and then we were quiet and just listened to the hail and the windshield wipers.

After a while Sam's mom asked me if I was okay. She was like "You okay honey?" and she was looking at me in the rearview mirror with lots of mercy. I nodded and tried to seem delicate. Then Sam turned the radio on to some Top 40 station and his mom turned it off and said "Not now Sammy I need to concentrate. Just play Snake or something" and Sam said "I've been playing Snake all day Moms. Give a brotha a break yo." I thought it was pretty funny how Sam was suddenly some homeboy.

Then Sam's mom looked at me in the rearview mirror again and asked me if anyone had touched me inappropriately and I shook my head and then she asked me if I got into a fight with my boyfriend and I shook my head again and then she asked me if I was absolutely sure that I didn't want to call anyone. She said I was more than welcome to use her cell phone and she had an iPhone and as soon as she held it up I had this instinct to take it P like thieving is in my blood now. I thought about calling you in Memphis but I was afraid my voice would give me away and then Sam's mom would know I was a boy. I know my voice isn't deep like the Major's or anything but it's not no GIRL'S voice that's for sure. I just shook my head again.

Every time Sam's mom glanced at me in the rearview mirror I looked down. I wondered what Branson would do in this situation. He would have probably wound up asking the mom to go see a movie with him or something crazy like that. He might've even asked her if he could put his testicles on her breasticles. He did that once P I swear. We were in front of the OMNIMAX theater on Water Avenue and this woman with long black hair walked by and he said "Excuse me miss" and then she stopped and turned around and she was like thirty-something. Branson said "Can I make put my testicles on your breasticles?" and she snorted at him and called him a menace and walked away. I think Branson really thought she might say yes because he was mad disappointed. Later I asked him what putting your testicles on somebody's breasticles meant but he just

just shook his head and said "You don't know SHIT Zilla!"

It had stopped hailing by the time we pulled into a Mobil station but it was raining again and even harder now like you couldn't even see it like it was coming at you from all sides like an army. Sam ran inside to go to the bathroom and his mom was about to get out to fill the car with gas when she turned to me and said "You're not pregnant are you?"

Even though I was shocked by her question I shook my head. I was so shocked that I sort of made a weird squeaking noise with my mouth which I think she misunderstood to mean that maybe I WAS PREGNANT because then she said "Sweetie if you are it's okay. I just need to know how I can help you."

I froze P.

She said "You must be so shaken up. Poor thing."

When she was pumping gas she called her husband on her iPhone. I could hear her pretty good through the window. That bump on her nose was really big. She said "We could let her stay in Katie's room. . . . Just a night or two. Katie's not coming home for a few weeks anyway. . . . The poor thing is terrified David. . . . Yeah just pull the extra comforter out of the trunk in the basement. . . . Maybe thirteen fourteen . . ."

After she hung up the phone she opened the front door and told me that something was wrong with her debit card and she had to go inside and deal with the attendant. She looked mad desperate with wet hair like she just got bit by a dog or something. She told me that she'd just spoken to her husband and how I was more than welcome to stay with them and how Sam's older sister Katie was away at school and how I could sleep in her room.

P for some reason there were tears in my eyes and I couldn't tell if I was acting or if they were real. Does that ever happen to you onstage? Like in a play or during a monologue? Do you get real tears? And if so do you feel weird about it like you're lying or like your soul is turning gray?

Sam's mom said she would be right back and closed the door and jogged into the Mobil station where I could see Sam playing one of those games with the mechanical claw where you try to make it grab a stuffed animal. I imagined his room full of toys and stuffed animals and LEGO villages and a big-ass X Box throne and my stomach started knotting up.

On the other side of the road there was a strip mall with a Mexican restaurant and a RadioShack and a karate studio and a quick-drop photo lab. All four places were closed and there wasn't a single car in the parking lot.

After Sam's mom paid for the gas she went over to Sam and watched him go for the stuffed animals. She bent down and tried to help him too. She was really rooting for him and I was impressed with her mothering skills.

That's when I grabbed his book bag. P you can call me a thief but that would be lame because you've known that about me for a while now. You'd have to call me something else to be original like a marauder. A marauder or like a bandit. I don't know what's inside me that allows me to do stuff like that. Do you think it's in our genes? Maybe Mom was some crazy shoplifter in her youth or maybe the Major does weird shit like steal a pack of breath mints when he's in line at the grocery store?

Anyway I reached into the side pocket of Sam's book bag and took his cell phone. It wasn't an iPhone it was a Sony Ericsson and I almost put it in my pocket but I couldn't because I knew someone would be able to trace it and plus I felt a little guilty about depriving him of his Snake game so I left it in the front seat and opened the door and made a dead sprint for the strip mall with his book bag. My head felt like it was going to split open every time my feet pushed off the pavement. There weren't any cars on the road which was probably the luckiest break I'd had till this Lincoln picked me up.

Behind the Mexican-food place there was a spot for shelter between these two big green recycling Dumpsters. I flipped their plastic lids backwards so they would form a roof. There was also this long cornfield back there and then a bunch of woods. In the middle of the cornfield there was an abandoned green Chevelle like one of those really old ones from the seventies and it had an orange sticker on the windshield and it was mostly rusted out and the tires had been slashed and the back windshield was busted to shit and someone had spray painted "THE ISH EATS SHIT" on the driver's side door. I figured I could try and wait the rain out a bit and then make a run for the car because it would be a good place to rest but NOT SLEEP and not get so wet and maybe it would be a little warmer than my spot underneath the Dumpster lids. The cornstalks weren't even a foot tall but there was like this SEA of the stuff P and with the rain going diagonal there was something ominous about it like the corn itself would start humming in some low warlock voice and swallow you up if you walked too far into it.

For at least an hour I sat under the little Dumpster roof with my knees pulled into my chest. My ass was wet and I was freezing and on top of all that I was suddenly freakishly paranoid that Sam's mom had called the cops like the Idaho State Smokeys or whatever they're called. I promised myself that if I heard anyone coming I would run for the cornfield despite my head wounds.

In Sam's book bag there were three pairs of boxer shorts and a pair of swimming trunks and a toothbrush and a tube of Crest toothpaste. In a separate compartment there was a thing of dental floss and two unopened Ocean Spray juice boxes and three pairs of white athletic socks and a pair of blue Adidas sweatpants. Also in another zipped pocket was a book called How to Survive A Robot Uprising: Tips on Defending Yourself Against the Coming Rebellion. On the cover was a giant silver robot with fighter planes and choppers swirling around it. From its red eyes it was shooting two death rays down at an ant-sized man who was running away.

I opened the book and this is what it said. I'm copying it word for word from the book.

HOW TO FOOL FACE RECOGNITION

A robot never forgets a face, so the best way to avoid recognition is never show yours. If a robot does catch a glimpse of your mug, it must compare you to a database of other faces in order to recognize you. Here's a variety of tricks to make sure you remain incognito in a world full of prying robot eyes.

+ STAY ALERT +

Cameras are passive sensors that can watch silently. Survey your surroundings for hidden cameras and remember where they are. They are usually placed high up. Mounted on top of buildings or at the top of light poles in parking lots. Be especially wary of pan-tilt-zoom cameras that move by themselves; their only purpose is to detect your face and zoom in on it.

+ DISGUISE YOUR FACE +

Use a mask to completely cover your face and hair, wear (or grow) facial hair, or don sunglasses or a wig. These layers will hide your facial features and gender, as well as the distinctive patterns of subdermal veins visible to hyperspectral cameras (which can see beneath your skin).

I flipped to another page and there was a piece of spiral notebook paper folded up. It was a letter from Sam to the author of the book and this is what he wrote I shit you not. I'll copy it word for word with all the punctuation.

Dear Mr. Wilson:

Your book is very excellent; in fact, one of the most excellent books I have ever read and I've read several books, mostly the Harry Potter books, which I have to say are fair to middling. I've even read an adult book by the accomplished writer Stephen King, although my mom took it away before I could finish it because she thought it was too advanced for my intellect. It was called <u>Christine</u> and it was about this haunted car and it was pure horror. But your book is better, I think, because it tells you what to do in case the robots come. And I think they will come because cell phones are so advanced and everyone has e-mail and so the codes are already in place. That makes a lot of sense to me, although my mother, who is fair to middling regarding these matters, thinks my imagination is over-inflamed.

I'm quite good at that game Snake, by the way. Do you think the robots are somehow monitoring me when I play this game? I hope not, although it would be interesting to meet one sometime, preferably a neutral robot who is more likely to be considerate to a human boy such as myself.

Well, I have to go now. I'll finish this letter when I get home. I'm currently at my cousin Larry's house. He is quite overweight, I think, and perhaps clinically depressed about it.

Your most feverish reader,
Samuel David Brock

How about that letter P? That kid Sam is like some computer nerd genius type who is all into the future. He'll probably grow up to be a scientist or he'll paint weird pictures of robots keeping humans as pets or something. Plus he used so much punctuation which I am bad at I admit like especially with commas. I never know where they're supposed to go or how many you're supposed to use so I pretty much just leave them out. I guess that makes me a grammar bandit too.

There was some other weird stuff in the book bag that I have to tell you about P and this is what I found it was a rubber Halloween mask and it was under the swimsuit. At first I was like does this kid SWIM with a Halloween mask on? I pulled it out and held it up and I'm holding it right now with my left hand and squeezing my spiral notebook between my legs and my teeth are still fucking chattering and I'm almost positive the rubber Halloween mask is supposed to be Keanu Reeves who was that guy from The Matrix.

So what I did was I put on the mask and walked out to the Chevelle and opened the door which was barely still attached. The thing was like clinging to the car with a few skinny cables. I slid into the driver's seat and sat back and watched the rain hit the front windshield. I thought how it hadn't stopped raining since I left Portland and how the only time it stopped was when it hailed and then it started raining right away again.

The rearview mirror had been ripped off so there was no real way I could see what I looked like with the mask on but that was sort of an awesome feeling like I wasn't ANYONE for a second like I could be ANYTHING under the mask like a ghost or a wolf boy with a dead bird in my pocket or some green mist.

Through the nostril holes I could smell the car which smelled rusty but it sort of smelled like hair spray too. I was expecting to find a dead body in the backseat but all there was were a few empty forties of beer with the labels torn off and a twenty-pound dumbbell and a TV Guide with some skeezer on the cover from that emergency-room show that Mom likes to watch Mr. Gray's Body Parts or whatever it's called and the skeezer is that Asian one with the big juicy fish lips.

I was about to start looking through the TV Guide when maybe one of the coolest things I've ever seen happened and I can't help but wonder if it's because I put the mask on and gained special powers or if I like became something else for a moment.

This is what I saw P it was a HUGE ANIMAL I shit you not and it walked right out into the middle of the field like I'm almost positive it came from the woods. At first I thought it was some sort of Sasquatch beast like Big Foot or Chewy from Star Wars or just some half-man creature whose mom was a human woman and dad was like a bear or a wild horse because it sort of reared up on its hind legs. When it went to all fours I could see that it was some sort of a deer only bigger and hairier. Maybe it was a moose or an elk? It definitely had antlers and it was seriously seriously humongously big P. It just stood there facing the Chevelle like it was talking to the car like it knew I was inside it and the beast creature and the Chevelle were having some freaky conversation! I thought it was going to walk up to the car and mad eat me P but it didn't. Instead it sort of jerked its head like it was paranoid too like maybe as much as me even and it ran off through the field and back into the woods. I thought it was so weird how it came out in the rain like that. I mean don't most animals hate the rain? Remember how Sarge would go hide under Edward's bed during thunderstorms and we would have to coax him out with Mom's leftover Hamburger Helper?

I have no explanation for nature that's for sure like animals and vegetables and minerals are completely mysterious categories as far as I'm concerned and rain and rocks and snow and tornadoes too. I mean God is a fucking trip right P? He invented so much weird shit like fish and Spanish and missiles and underground caves and machines that make cars and faces on the sides of mountains! And nudity and Venezuela and flying squirrels with fangs! And we have to deal with ALL OF IT ALL THE TIME!

I sat in the Chevelle and I was going to wait out the rain and really try and REST and NOT SLEEP and maybe stop my thoughts from SPIRALING OUT OF CONTROL but I kept getting this mad paranoid feeling that those forties of beer in the backseat were Budweisers and that they belonged to those ingrates who jumped me back at the bus station which really wasn't that far away from where I was when I really thought about it and I kept getting this creepy feeling that they were going to show up any minute with like a staple gun or a noose or some sort of cattle prong and take me into the Mexican restaurant through the back where the grill is and torture me or cut one of my hands off and fry it up with hot peppers and make me eat it with some guacamole and chips or something. I know that's insane P and it's a good argument for me getting back on my medication but I really believed that I really really did. Talk about mental illness right? After I find you in Memphis and everything works out and you don't die I'm going to call a cab and have it drive me straight to the first mental hospital I can find.

I got out of the Chevelle and sort of zigzagged through the cornfield in the rain. I had Sam's book bag and I was still wearing the Keanu Reeves mask mainly because I didn't want those dudes who jumped me to know who I was. It was like they were robots from the book and I was trying to confuse them by changing my identity. So I rolled up my jeans and took my New Balances and socks off and stuck them in the book bag and ran barefoot like a maniac through the goopy mud. I kept having this very real feeling that one of those robots was marching behind me so just to distract myself I started saying the General George S. Patton Junior Prayer that I learned at Buckner the one I wrote to you about earlier and I have to admit P it somehow helped. Even though it was STILL RAINING and it was starting to get dark and my feet were killing me and my head was still pounding and the ringing in my brain was getting louder that prayer helped.

I vowed that I would never turn away from help again and I started thinking about how I could've been in a nice house and like totally sleeping in some girl's bed all warm and dry and probably taking a shower and washing my hair with some expensive shampoo that smells like peaches or cherries or fresh apple pie or something. It almost makes me sick to my stomach as I'm writing this even though I'm safe and dry now in the backseat of this Lincoln.

I eventually made it through the field just before it went completely dark. Then there was another highway. It was a pretty busy one with semis roaring by so I decided to just sit down on the shoulder. I eventually took the mask off because I figured no one would stop for some kid wearing a rubber Halloween mask in the beginning of March. I sat close to the zooming cars because I figured the sound of their blaring horns would help me stay awake and NOT SLEEP. Either that or I wouldn't be able to fight sleep anymore and someone would veer off the road and put me out of my misery for good. I was really at that place P. Just a few hours ago. I was so exhausted I didn't even care if a COP caught me. If that happened I knew I would be taken in and eventually Mom and the Major would get called and then I'd have to face the shitty music and under the circumstances even THAT seemed okay. Have you ever been at the end of your rope like that P? I mean you probably are now right because of your cancer but maybe you're way more professional or poised when it comes to that kind of exhaustion? Or maybe you DO feel it too? Like you're always running away from everything and you're hungry and your pants keep almost falling down because they got your only belt buckle which was one of your favorite items from Portland and you have no friends and everyone thinks you're a fucking girl and you suck at most things mainly Monday drill and decision making and other important leadership qualities and you don't know if you're going to suddenly puke or piss your pants or if you'll get lucky enough to find a safe place to sleep? That's what I was going through earlier P. Exactly that and God is a dick for letting all of this happen! He's a fucking dick for letting you have cancer and if he had an e-mail address I would get a Yahoo account or one of those other free ones and fire off a few complaints because as it stands right now there's no way I'm going to Heaven anyway if that place even EXISTS if God is even OUT THERE the great miracle maker!

When the Lincoln Town Car pulled up Dave

or Dan or Dale lowered the window and asked me if I needed a ride and I said yes and he said he was heading east so I got in. I told him how I was supposed to be on a bus heading to Memphis and how I got jumped and how they took my money and how I wasn't feeling so great. Then he offered me a piece of gum and I took it and as soon as I bit into it I almost puked I don't even know why maybe because of the sudden rush of flavor but I swallowed hard and kept chewing. Then the old lady in the passenger's seat turned around to look at me and she was staring at me hard like she could barely make me out like she was mad confused about something. I said "I'm a boy okay?" and this is what the old leaky-eyed hag said back and it's the only thing she said the whole time I've been in this car P she said "I don't care what you are shrimp" and then she turned around just like that. She called me a fucking shrimp P! She was the exact kind of person I would have robbed in Forest Park I swear.

A few minutes after she called me a shrimp the guy who was driving asked me to buckle my seat belt and I did and then he stared at me through the rear-view mirror a bit and asked me what school I went to and I told him about Buckner and how it's a military school. He said "You on spring break?" and I said "Till next week" which was my first lie. I tried not to say much after that because I was afraid that I would just start lying like crazy like a bunch of loose teeth falling out of your mouth or something.

I have to stop writing now P because my hand really is hurting pretty bad and I'm not just saying that. It's like I have a permanent headache in my palm. And this pen is running out so it may be a while before I can write you again. I'm just glad I'm not dead and that I'm finally out of the rain.

I hope you're okay and not in too much pain.

I remember seeing this movie where a guy gets AIDS and dies. He gets all these brown spots on his face and starts stumbling around his apartment and then he goes blind and collapses on a coffee table.

Is anything like that happening to you yet? I figure AIDS and cancer have at least a few things in common but maybe I'm totally wrong. When I get to you you better not be blind. At least give me a few days of you being able to see.

Love,
Your Bro

August 28th, 2007

Dear New Boy,

Welcome to Buckner!

This is my fifth year at the academy. As a seventh-grader in New Haven, Connecticut, I coasted by with a 3.0 GPA, played sports, and was fine with being "good enough." Then I came to Buckner's summer camp and after the incredible experience I had, my parents decided to enroll me for the full academy program.

My experiences here at Buckner have been life-changing, as I'm sure they will be for you, too. The program has taught me dedication and motivation. I've learned that anything I want to do can be accomplished with hard work. My cumulative GPA is now 3.8, and I tutor other cadets in math at the Reginald Plotke Learning Center. This year I will compete in three sports: football, basketball, and track. I've been challenged with the leadership position of captain of the varsity basketball team and have worked very hard in preparation for the upcoming season. Chapel services help ground me. I listen to each message to see how it applies to my everyday life.

In our Leadership Education Training classes, I've learned alternative methods of dealing with problems and people and strategic ways to talk to and motivate others. I've earned several medals and academic stars, but my coveted achievement is the JROTC National Scholar Athlete Medal because it is awarded to a cadet who is successful both in sports and in the classroom.

All this is here for you, too. As you begin the difficult initiation process that will challenge you during the coming weeks, just know that I was once in your shoes. Have faith that Buckner Academy is here to make you better!

Sincerely,

Captain Patrick Karl
Commander, Bravo Company

September 10, 2007

Dear Mom,

So I promised you I would write you so here goes my first letter. I got here two days ago and I haven't slept yet. This place is really scary Mom. Not like horror movie scary the kind of scary where you think you might die because you don't have what it takes. All the buildings are made out of stone and there's this huge graveyard full of these things called class stones and my room overlooks it and I keep thinking I'm going to see the Headless Horseman galloping through with an axe or something. I know Dad is a military hero and Edward won all those physical-fitness badges and is an all-conference wrestler and can do that thing where you grab a pole and stick your legs out sideways but I don't think I have the same intestinal fortitude or whatever that's called. What I'm saying Mom is that I'm weaker than everybody like physically and mentally too like I can't remember how to ask permission to eat or use the bathroom. I screw everything up. I feel like I've been shining shoes nonstop. My squad leader hates me. He's this guy Sergeant Voyce and every time he sees me he makes me drop and do push-ups. I know I should give it more time but I was wondering if I could come home. I really don't think I'm cut out for this Mom. I know that's disappointing to hear but I'm just trying to be honest. If you let me come home I promise I won't smoke any more pot and I won't steal anything and I'll stop doing antihistamines and I'll apply myself in school and start using my intelligence in a positive way. Things are so bad that last night in the middle of the night I had to go to the bathroom really bad but I didn't go because there was this guy on duty who likes to poke me in the Adam's apple with his knuckle. He's done it like six times in two days his name is Staff Sergeant Rebillard and he has a face like a smashed cat so I stayed in bed and eventually fell asleep but I pissed my bed right before reveille. It wasn't a huge amount or anything it was mostly my underwear and pajama bottoms I threw them away but I had to change my sheets before first mess which meant that I couldn't work on my shoes and they weren't shiny enough and Sergeant Voyce wound up making me stay in push-up position for the whole morning formation and my hands wouldn't stop shaking all through breakfast if you don't let me come home I think I'm going to run away like go AWOL and never look back or maybe I'll stick a fork in my eye and get kicked out I swear Mom I'm going to do that if you loved me you would let me come home. Okay fuck this I just read this letter and there's no way I'm sending it to you. No way no way no way no way. It will live in this notebook forever or I will burn it.

September 25th, 2007

Dear Jamie,

How's military school? I hope it's going well. You've been gone for almost a month and it's strange getting used to you not being here. At night every time I look over at your bed I keep expecting to hear you snoring or talking in your sleep like you do, but you're not there. Do you keep your new roommate up at night with your snoring? Has he written down some of the things you say in your sleep? Remember that time after we went fishing in Michigan how you stood straight up in your bed and said that the state capital of Ohio was hidden in the cornflakes? That was really funny. You should tell your new roommate to keep a pen and a pad of paper near his bed so he can write everything down.

Things at home are good. I just applied for early acceptance into the University of Chicago premed program. I applied to Yale and Carnegie Mellon too, but my first choice would be U of C because it's the best. My biology teacher, Mr. Sparr, thinks I have a great chance to get in all three, so cross your fingers for me.

I decided to join the cross-country team because I thought it would get me in better shape for wrestling. Three-point-one miles is no joke. After the two-mile mark I always feel like I have nothing left. You have to really dig down deep for that final one-point-one. I'm going to try to go down a weight class this year because Coach Calhoun thinks I could win state at 156. I'm on a no-cholesterol, high-protein diet. I mostly eat oatmeal and almonds and salmon. Did you know that salmon is considered one of the perfect foods? Apparently so is anything from a goat, like goat milk or goat cheese. And coconut water is the most hydrating thing you can put in your body. Did you know that? It's even more hydrating than Gatorade. Dad's basically on the same diet, so it makes it easy for Mom.

Speaking of Mom, she's on a mission to renovate the basement. She was on the phone with Home Depot for over an hour today. She ordered a bunch of paneling for the walls and she's getting carpeting too. She spends most of her time down there, sorting through old boxes and trying to figure out where she's going to put stuff. Dad wants a bar down there, too. And maybe a sauna and a Jacuzzi. Don't be surprised if they put you to work during your Thanksgiving break.

I got these circular push-up mounts that the Navy Seals use for their workouts. They're part of the perfect push-up package that I ordered off the Internet. I've been working out with them for two weeks now and my chest and shoulders are getting really strong. I asked Mom to get you a pair so you could do some working out on the side. I know you don't like the notion of fitness so much, but it could help you get through the initiation process for new cadets that Dad was telling me about. I also got a pull-up bar mounted in our room now. I've been doing three sets of ten three times a week and I'm hoping to get up to twelve by next week.

Jamie, I wanted you to know one thing. Remember how you were getting into all that trouble this summer? With the stealing and that thing you did to Mrs. Weitzel's birdbath? And how I walked in on you smoking pot in the garage? Well, I never said anything about that to Mom or Dad. I let that one stay between us. I hope you believe me, Jamie, because it's true. I know we haven't always gotten along, but I don't want you to think for a minute that I'm some sort of narc.

But regarding your recent behavior, I do hope that Buckner is helping you find a better path, one that is more productive and helping you move toward your potential, because you have so much of that, Jamie, so much potential. All three of us do, and even though Peter is squandering his down in Memphis or Athens, Georgia, or wherever it is that he is busy being an opinionated homosexual, there is still hope for you.

Please don't break Mom and Dad's hearts.

Please do not do that, Jamie.

Love,
Edward

March 8, 2008

Dear P,

It's two days since I wrote you and my hand is definitely starting to feel better. My head hurts less too but it still throbs if I bend down to tie my shoes. When I do anything like that it feels like my eyeballs are going to burst.

I'm at this shitty little place called the Lakeside Motel where Dan or Dave or Dale and the old lady with the leaky eye dropped me off it's about twenty miles away from Highway 25 on this road with this huge old parking lot where all these semis and a bunch of truck drivers are smoking and sitting on plastic beach chairs and drinking out of bottles with brown paper bags over them and playing cards and talking on their cell phones. It's mad big this parking lot thing and there's a hamburger stand blaring classic rock at the front like mostly Bruce Springsteen and Fleetwood Mac and Pink Floyd. I was walking around there a little earlier but there weren't any other kids around. It's like truckers have something against the younger generation. This one Mexican dude with all these tattoos on his arms offered me an ear of corn on a stick. He had like a whole bucket-ful of them but I said no thanks and kept weaving through the crowd. In some ways that parking lot is like a carnival without rides. A carnival without rides or kids. I think it used to be a drive-in-movie place because there's an old white screen with all these stains on it. Someone spray painted "JESUS HAS A WEBSITE" on it which is a funny thing to write without adding the website address like it's some seriously privileged information that you have to PRAY to get or something.

I'm writing to you from a picnic table behind the motel. I'm under this ancient tree with maroon-colored leaves. There's a huge spiderweb from the tree that attaches to the motel and I keep waiting for some big hairy spider to come out like a tarantula or a black widow or one of those giant camel spiders from the Iraq war like one of the ones E showed me on his computer before I left for Buckner. Anyway P it's a pretty artistic-looking web and there are like five flies trapped in it and one of them is really strug-gling to get free and I have to admit that I'm sort of getting off on it like I can't wait for the spider to come and eat all the flies and maybe torture one just for pleasure.

Next to the picnic table is this little swimming pool. It has a diving board and there are a few lounge chairs scattered around it but there's a NO SWIMMING sign and there are all of these dead things floating in it like mice and bugs and frogs and the water is all murky and green and looks like sewage. There's probably a bunch of snakes wriggling around under the surface too. I wouldn't go in it if you paid me a thousand bucks.

I'm not exactly sure what town I'm in but I'm somewhere near Buffalo Wyoming. There's no lake near the Lakeside Motel. At least not one that I can see so I think the motel must be built on a foundation of bullshit. Maybe there used to be some prehistoric lake where the dinosaurs used to bathe or swim and it dried up and they filled it with dirt and trees or something? Or maybe the person's last name who owns the motel is Lakeside like John Lakeside or Kevin Lakeside or Rodrigo Lakeside?

When I said good-bye to Dave or Dan or Dale and the old lady with the leaky eye not much happened. I was hoping they would offer me some cash or a box of Slim Jims or like a gift certificate to McDonald's or something but they didn't. Dale or Dan or Dave DID wind up buying me some waffles at a Denny's though so I finally got to eat which was cool but I got diarrhea pretty bad and almost ruined a rest stop bathroom. There was only one stall in that bathroom and this little black kid was waiting to use it and now he'll probably hate white people.

Back in the Lincoln I wound up falling asleep for like four hours. For a second I thought maybe Dan or Dave or Dale and the old lady with the leaky eye tried to poison me because people carry vials P. They carry vials and put little pellets of cyanide between your pancakes when you're not looking. I had never felt that sleepy before in my life.

When I woke up we were stopped at a traffic light in a small town and the old lady with the leaky eye was staring at me. She was completely turned around in her seat with her face sort of perched on the top of the headrest. I was like "What?" and she said "You got one heckuva snore on you shrimp" and then she sort of imitated me snoring and I have to admit it was funny P.

Anyway they wound up dropping me off at the Lakeside Motel and I'll probably never see them again.

I didn't have enough money for a room because

it's forty-two bucks a night and I only have eleven left. I thought I could just hang out in the lobby and crash on the sofa till the girl behind the counter got sick of me. For a while she was pretty talkative and maybe even sexually obsessed with me. Her name was Erin and she wasn't too pretty but I would have probably let her give me a hand job. She had these big sad eyes and pimples along her hairline and this nose ring that you could barely see like a little speck of glass stuck to her nostril.

Erin's mom and dad owned the motel and she was on spring break from college and she was pissed because most of her friends were at some resort town in South Carolina called Myrtle Beach and her parents made her come home to help out at the motel. She said she was fine with it though because everyone gets mad herpes in that resort town. Herpes and crabs and this other sexually transmitted disease that makes you get lockjaw.

Another fact about Erin was that she was a freshman at North Carolina University and she wouldn't stop talking about their men's basketball team and how even though they lost some players to the NBA draft that they were going to win the national championship at the end of the month. She was wearing a light blue North Carolina hoodie and even her keychain had "TAR HEELS" on it. Man P skeezers who love sports are not cool in my opinion. Edward would have probably loved Erin for that very reason. She had pretty nice titties to be fair. I never got too good a look at her ass because her hoodie was hanging down over it. It made me curious to see it though which scientifically speaking is an effective technique that other girls should try. Erin's best feature was her hair. It was even better than her titties. It was the color of butterscotch pudding. E would have definitely been into her P. I can just picture them walking around back in Cincinnati like at Eastgate Mall like holding hands and eating one of those big soft pretzels with mustard on it.

Erin was watching TV in the office. I think it was a DVD of some shark movie from the nineties starring LL Cool J. I kept having this weird fantasy that she would lift her hoody and flash me but things like that never really happen right? At least to me they don't. I'm sure guys like Brad Pitt and Leonardo DeCaprio and LL Cool J get that kind of special treatment from mad West Coast skeezers but you have to win an Oscar or be voted sexiest male spy of the decade to earn those sorts of privileges. I'll probably wind up dating some shy girl with a neck brace and an ass shaped like a stop sign and she'll NEVER lift her hoodie for me not even if I pay her.

Erin let me use the bathroom in the little motel office and I tried to take a mini-shower in the sink which is something I did a lot in Portland because the community shower on the fourth floor of Washington House always had trash in it like a half-eaten burrito or a paper plate with ketchup on it or something. Once there was this old man sitting down on the shower room floor. He was naked and his chest was all saggy and bald and he was clipping his toenails. When I walked in he said "THERE'S my community!" He like totally shouted it at the top of his lungs so I turned around and went back to my room.

In the motel office bathroom there was a real bar of soap none of that pink squirty stuff. I washed my face and wet my hair down and gargled some cold water and changed into a pair of Sam's sweat socks which actually fit me pretty good. I was really start-ing to feel better even though my scalp itched and my teeth felt coated with germs.

When I came out Erin had turned off the TV

and started acting suspicious. First she said "Did you just shoot up in there because if you're like shooting up or doing crack or something I'm going to have to ask you to leave." I told her I didn't do anything and then she said "Well did you like SNORT something?" and I told her I just washed up a little and I showed her how my hair was wet but she still wouldn't believe me so I pulled up my sleeves to prove I didn't have track marks and then she put on some lip gloss and asked if someone was coming to pick me up and I said "No" and she said "You just like hanging out in motels?" and I said "Maybe" and then she crossed her arms and said "Are you like homeless? Because no offense or whatever but you sort of smell like you are."

My face got hot with embarrassment and now I live in terror about having BO total terror P but I figure it could have been my jeans because they tend to get smelly. They would get that way especially in Portland because I didn't wash my clothes much there.

I told Erin the skeezer that I wasn't fucking homeless and how I was on my way to seeing you and how I had been on that Greyhound and got jumped in Idaho and how I had to hitch a ride with Sam and his mom and another one with Dale or Dan or Dave and the old lady with the leaky eye who kept calling me shrimp and Erin was like "If you're gonna lie you should be more creative."

I swore to her I wasn't lying and showed her my puffy eye and the scrapes behind my ear and she said it didn't prove anything and then she asked me my age and I told her the truth and she said I was younger than fourteen and that pissed me off and I didn't even bother telling her that I'm going to be FIFTEEN in like nine days. I didn't even bother because I had decided right then and there that she wasn't worth it. It's weird P just when you start telling people the truth they don't believe you. I have to remember that I do.

Then she said "Why do you dye your hair are you tryin to change your identity or something?" and I told her I liked it black and she was like "You're obviously SO blond. You should get your roots touched up" and then I said "I'm not a fucking girl okay?" and she said "For a minute there I wasn't exactly sure so thanks for clearing that up."

Man I had a desperate urge for a cigarette right then. A desperate desperate urge P. I asked her if she really was confused about my gender and she said she thought I might be "some little dyke-job from Gillette looking to hook up."

Then I said this P I said "Do you wanna see it?" meaning my dick and she KNEW I meant my dick because you could see it on her face. I don't mean you could see my DICK on her face I mean you could see how she knew what I was talking about on her face. I swear I said that P and it made me feel so much better.

She stared at me for a second and said "Look I don't care if you stay here but my mom is coming back in like an hour and she won't be cool with some homeless kid or whatever you are just like setting up camp in the office. This is around the time we start to get customers. In fact in about twenty minutes a bunch of those truckers down the road are gonna start getting rooms."

She was pretty mean when she said all of that but then she sort of went soft and said that I should go hang out behind unit seven because her mom never went back there. I asked her why her mom never went back there and she said it was because last year some trucker from Fort Collins Colorado hung himself from the copper birch which is the tree I'm sitting under as I write this P the one with the maroon leaves and the spiderweb! How spooky is that! I keep thinking I'll look up and see the ghost of that trucker in the branches with a noose around his neck or like a fucking raven perched on his shoulder.

Then Erin said she had to go restock the candy machine and left through the back of the office. I was seriously tempted to see if there was any cash behind the front desk like in a cigar box or just in some drawer but I didn't want to push my luck.

I was about to go find unit seven when this weird guy wearing a black silky on his head came in through the front door. He was dressed pretty normal with jeans and a plain white T-shirt and a pair of white Nike Air Force 1s. He was really skinny and his face was all pale and oily. He said "Is Erin around?" His voice was high and sort of gayish-seeming but I don't mean that in a bad way P it's more of a scientific observation. What I mean to say is that I'm pretty sure some homosexuals sound more like women than men wouldn't you agree being one yourself? I've even heard some in Portland who sounded like they were from England.

I told him that Erin just went to go restock the candy machine and he said "The Blakes get all over you if you're late paying your bill." I asked him who the Blakes were and he said they were the owners of the motel and that Erin was their daughter. He said he actually liked the dad whose name was Jerry but that Erin and her mom were ruthless little bitches and they would start sliding notes under your door if you were late paying your bill. Then he said "I'm Lewis by the way" and we did a normal handshake. I was expecting him to be all limp in the wrist but his grip was firm like almost as firm as the Major's I shit you not P.

Lewis told me he had lived at the motel for six months and that he kept expecting the Blakes to cut him a break with a cheaper month-to-month plan but that it never happened and then he asked me my name and I told him and he pulled out a pack of Marlboros and I didn't even need to ask he just sensed my desperation and offered one and said "Yep that's me. Supporting the youth of America. Guilty as charged." And then he lit me with a cheap Bic.

After we smoked for a minute he asked me if my dad was one of the truckers down the road and I said no and then he asked me if I was related to the Blakes and I said no again and then he said "Who are you like one of Fagan's boys?" but I had no idea what he was talking about and he told me about some movie called Oliver and said it was one of the greatest movies ever made and that he learned more watching that movie than he did "moving up the glorious ranks of the Nevada public school system and matriculating to Colorado College" whatever that meant. The cigarette tasted so good I felt like I wouldn't have to eat for a week.

Then Lewis said "You're not from Wyoming I gather?" and I almost told him I was from Cincinnati but I couldn't because I was suddenly feeling racy like I really needed my medication to focus on what was right in front of me and I hadn't felt that for weeks P I shit you not. He said "Don't be nervous I'm just a harmless country boy from Effingham Illinois" and I told him I thought he already said he was from Nevada and he went "I was born in Tidewater Florida spent my youth in the middle of Illinois and my adolescence and early adulthood in Reno Nevada. It's sounds complicated I'm the first one to admit it but fear not" and I said "Who said I was afraid of you?" and he was like "Ooh toughness I like toughness. Wish I had a little more of that myself" and then he made me feel guilty about him giving me a cigarette and said something about how the least I could do was engage in some small talk with my fellow man so I told him how I was in Portland and then we smoked some more and then I told him he was weird-looking and he said "Weird's not always a bad thing." Then I asked him why he wore the silky and he said it helped keep the bugs out of his hair and then I told him he looked weird again. I'm not sure why I had to say it twice. He was like "You're from Portland and you've never seen a guy like me before? Where'd you live in the planetarium?" and then I told him how I wasn't FROM Portland but how I just lived there for a while.

He made smoke rings and I thought it was weird how he might be gay but was doing such a macho thing. Remember how the Major used to make smoke rings before Mom got him to quit smoking the Lucky Strikes? How he would do three of them and then blow out the third one and how Mom would wave them away but it would be like she was sort of flirting with him? That was probably the only time they seemed like they actually liked each other.

Lewis leaned toward me all concerned and said

"What happened to your eye anyway?" and I told him how I got jumped by those punks in Idaho and he made a concerned face and asked if they took my money and I said they got most of it and how I had to hitch a ride and got dropped off at the motel. It sucked having to tell that whole story AGAIN. Then he asked me if I had a place to stay and I said I didn't and he said I was more than welcome to stay with him and how he had two twin beds that were pushed together but that it would be no trouble for him to pull them apart.

P I looked hard at Lewis. I had to because I'm at the point now where I don't trust anyone. I felt pretty sorry for him with his skinny arms and his oily face and his weird voice. He seemed really lonely but not in some perverted Alan Skymer way. At Washington House there was this old gay man who Branson called Sweet Larry and he would always try and get one of us to go up to his room with him by offering us free long-distance use on his phone and microwave dinners. Sweet Larry was fifty-something and had dyed hair and wore yellow aviator sunglasses and the same blue tank top every day. Sometimes he would point a finger gun at you and shoot it at you like he was hunting. He did it to Branson all the time but Branson would say "Yeah you wish Sweet Larry." One time this kid named Diesel agreed to go up in his room because he thought he could steal Sweet Larry's Tivo. Sweet Larry gave him a turkey sandwich and some French wine and Diesel wound up falling asleep on his sofa and when he woke up Sweet Larry was standing over him and jerking off and whimpering. When I looked hard at Lewis I had a gut feeling he wasn't like that. Even though he looked a little weird he seemed like a decent person.

I said "You aren't some pervert are you?" and he looked me square in the face and said "I promise you I'm no pervert."

His room was more like an apartment than a motel room with a mini-refrigerator and a micro-wave oven and this little stove-top thing and pictures on the walls and plants on the air-conditioner thing and a pretty nice sound system.

Over his bed was a poster of that actress Scarlett Johansson. Do you know her P? She was in The Prestige if you ever saw that weird-ass movie. Anyway Lewis had a big poster of her above his bed so my theory about him being gay was definitely up in the air. If he was really gay he would have had a poster of Usher or Johnny Depp or some pretty dude with big eyelashes.

After Lewis pulled the beds apart he put new sheets on the one I was going to sleep in and then he asked me if I was hungry and I said I was starving so he cooked two Swanson Salisbury steak dinners in the microwave and gave me a can of cream soda.

Before he started to eat he took this little machine out of a black bag and pricked his finger and squeezed some blood on a tab thing and inserted the tab thing in the machine. Then he pulled out what looked like a big white pen and stuck himself in the side with it like right through his shirt and pressed this button thing at the top of the pen.

I asked him if he was a junkie and he told me he was a diabetic and that he was shooting insulin into his side and that the machine thing was a device called a glucometer that measured the sugar in his blood so he would know how much insulin he would need. When we started eating I asked him how many times a day he had to shoot that stuff into his side and he said four or five and I asked him if it hurt and he said you get used to it like anything else. I was impressed because he didn't even wince when he stuck himself P. I can't stand needles. Just the thought of them makes me feel tense. Lewis was way tougher than he looked.

P the microwave dinner was the best thing I ever tasted. I think it was probably because it was the first thing I'd eaten since Dale or Dave or Dan bought me those waffles and my taste buds were mad amped for some flavor. Lewis could've served me some dog food and I would have probably loved it.

After I was almost finished Lewis said he had two more microwave dinners and that I could have another one so I nodded and he nuked one. He was turning out to be really cool.

While eating the second microwave dinner I asked him why he lived in the motel and he said it was where he felt comfortable and then I asked him if he had family somewhere and he said his mom lived in Topeka Kansas and that his dad was "roaming around somewhere out there" and that they didn't speak. And then I asked him if he had any kids and he said he didn't and that the motel was a "transitional place" and I was like "From what to what?" and then he put his fork down and took a deep breath and blew it out all serious and said that he barely knew me and that I might want to run out of his room screaming but that it wouldn't be the first time it freaked someone out and he pointed to the door and told me if I needed to leave that it wasn't locked but to be careful with the screen door on the other side of the regular door because it tended to get stuck. I thought he was going to tell me he had just gotten out of prison for murder or rape or armed robbery or something.

But this is what he said P he said "I had top surgery a few months ago" and I was totally confused I was like "What's top surgery?" and he said he'd had his breasts removed and had had some reconstructive work done to help form his new chest and I said "You mean you had titties?" and he said yes he did but that he preferred to call them breasts.

P as you can see this was turning out to be one of the weirdest conversations I've ever had. I said "So you were like BORN with boobs?" and he said that he was born a woman and I said "So you're like a drag queen?" and he said "Not even remotely" and that he was someone who came into the world a woman and is transitioning to becoming a man. He said a drag queen is a man who likes to dress up in women's clothes and a drag KING is a woman who likes to dress up in MEN'S clothes and wear fake mustaches and put cowboy boots on and perform a lot of karaoke. I said "So you're not a drag ANYTHING?" and he said "There isn't a cell of drag to be found where Lewis Williams is concerned."

P I had to stop eating because I was so stunned.

Then I asked him when he decided he wanted to be a man and he said he made the decision after he got back from Iraq meaning the war meaning the first one back in the early nineties. He said back then he was known as Private First Class Louise Mills. This was a seriously crazy mind fuck P. I had met a lot of freaky people in Portland but no one like this. Then I asked him if he killed anyone in the war and he said no that he trained for it but mostly did administrative work in an office far away from the action.

What was weird P and I mean REALLY FUCK-ING WEIRD was that even though Lewis just told me he used to be a woman and had his titties removed I really believed he was a man. And the more I talked to him the more it seemed that way.

I asked him when he had the top surgery and he said three years ago and then I asked him if it was expensive and he said it was and he wouldn't tell me the amount and he talked about how hard it is to find a doctor who will even do it and how insurance companies won't cover the operation and how it totally wiped him out financially and how he put his life's savings toward it and even had to sell his car and that's why he lives in a cheap motel.

Then I was like "Do your parents know?" and he said his mom knew and that she was doing the best she could with it and how he was raised Roman Catholic like us P and how the church isn't too supportive of "gender transitional people." He said he and his mom talk a few times a month and that she's really trying. Then I asked him about his dad and he said that they haven't spoken in over fifteen years and it made me think of you and the Major and how that's what's happening to me and the Major too and how maybe that's what happens to all dads and sons except for maybe E and the Major.

We were quiet for a minute and you could hear some of those truckers Erin was talking about walking around outside and playing radios. Then Lewis said how he really wanted to start taking T but how his blood was already too messed up from the diabetes and how he couldn't quit smoking to save his life which was the worst thing a type A diabetic could do. I asked him what T was and he said it was testosterone as in the male hormone. I said "You take it so you can like grow a dick or something?" and he said

T won't grow you a dick but it does other things like changes your body in subtler ways like you start to get facial hair and your voice gets deeper and you get more aggressive.

Then I asked him if he wanted a dick and he said that it would be the ultimate goal and that there was an operation but that you could only afford it if you won "the flipping lottery" and he really said flipping instead of fucking and that reminded me of something Mom would do like when she wants to say shit but she says sugar foot instead.

Lewis took out his pack of Marlboros and gave me one and lit us and we both smoked. I have to admit I was eyeing his Salisbury steak dinner P because he hadn't finished it and I was still starving even after eating two of them but instead of asking for the steak I asked him why he wanted to be a man and he said "Because that's how I see myself. That's how I've always felt on the inside." Then I asked him if he thought I looked like a girl and he said that I have "softer features than your average bear" but that I definitely ACTED like a boy.

Man that was a relief to hear P. I mean Lewis probably has like superpowers when it comes to figuring these things out right? It was definitely a relief.

Then I asked him a totally crazy question P but it just came out and I was genuinely curious about it like in a totally scientific way and this is what I said I was like "When you were a woman did you slay lots of men?" and he said "Slay?" and I said "Fuck" and he was cool about it. He said he was with some men but that he found that he actually preferred women. I said "So you're like a lesbian" and he said "At the time I guess I was technically a lesbian yes."

I asked him if he had a girlfriend and he said that he did for a while but that she left him after his top surgery and how it took him by surprise but that it happens. He said her name was Anne and that she lived in Canada with another woman.

I said "So she really must have missed your titties" which was a rude thing to say P I realize it now. Lewis even got mad and said "please call them breasts" and I said "Breasts. Sorry."

Then Lewis told me about when he and Anne spoke about him becoming a man and how she was so supportive and how they had made all sorts of plans for the future like they were even talking about getting married with a traditional wedding in a church with a priest and a big white cake and everything but how the grossness of the top surgery really freaked her out. He said the early recovery is mad brutal and how his flesh was inflamed for a long time and how he had to fight off an infection. Then one day he came home and she was gone.

I asked him if he thought she would come back and he said no and that he's moving on and that that's life. Then I pointed to that actress in the poster that Scarlett Johansson skeezer and I went "You like her?" and this is what Lewis said P I shit you not he said "If I had a dick I would fuck her six ways to Sunday" and then we both started laughing like crazy. Lewis sort of honked when he laughed like he was part duck or something. I had never heard a laugh like that.

He finished his cigarette before me and put it out in an ashtray. I asked him if he had a job and he said how he was living off his veteran's pension and how the top surgery set him back a bit with the healing process and losing Anne. Then I asked him what he wanted to do and he said that he had a degree in history and that he wanted to get back into teaching. It turns out that when he was a woman he used to teach high school after he got back from Iraq. He was Ms. Mills and he taught history at some Catholic school in Illinois.

Then I said "How old are you anyway?" because I was really curious. I couldn't figure it out at all. He said "You go right for the jugular don't you? I'm thirty-six."

Then I told him how you were twenty-seven and he asked about you and I told him your name and how you were a playwright and what your plays are about like about how fucked up the government is and how George Bush is a clown and how you had that one play about the leader of England called Blair Which Project? and how you used a bunch of spray paint in it and spray painted like forty-some boxes of Nabisco shredded wheat. He asked where you lived and I told him how you were in Memphis and how we're from Cincinnati.

And then I told him what's going on P. I told him about Buckner and Portland and being on the run and then I told him about how I was trying to get to you because of how you're dying of cancer. When I heard myself say it out loud things got really fucked up and I like started punching myself like in my face and in my neck and I was suddenly crying like crazy in that way that makes it really hard to breathe it was almost like I was drowning but Lewis wrapped me up pretty quick and man he was stronger than I thought. He wrapped his arms around me and just sort of brought me to the ground and held me and I was panting and my head was throbbing and I thought I was going to throw up in my mouth and I couldn't seem to catch my breath. He just held me like that for a minute and then he said "Is your brother with your family?" and after like ten breaths I told him how you were with your boyfriend and I told him about Jorge and about you two being gay lovers I hope that's cool P. I know how some people like to keep their relationships on the down low but I figured Lewis was cool. We were still on the floor and we both wound up sitting there sort of Indian-style like we were about to play duck-duck-goose or something. And then I told him about Mom and the Major and about E and about how I ran away from Buckner and we smoked like four more cigarettes and he put this band on called Wolf Parade that I had never heard before but I liked them a lot and then a few minutes later more of those truckers I was telling you about started coming over from that parking lot and there was a knock on the door and Lewis answered it and this guy who wasn't a trucker came in and Lewis scored some weed that came in this little plastic terrarium and then the guy left and we wound up getting really stoned like it was maybe the best weed I've ever smoked in my life. Man I really think you would love this guy P. I mean I realize he might not be totally a GUY yet like in a medical way but you would definitely like him.

Later I fell asleep in the bed he made for me and when I woke up I took a shower for the first time in days and I brushed my teeth with his extra toothbrush and he made me breakfast. It was French toast on the little stove-top thing he has and now I'm sitting at this picnic table in the back of the motel beside the big tree with the maroon leaves and that spiderweb and the little shitty pool with the floating mice and frogs and I keep thinking I'm going to see the ghost of that trucker from Colorado.

But I just wanted to write and let you know that I'm finally feeling pretty safe and that I think I made my first real friend since I left Portland.

Lewis said I could use his motel room phone to call you later so I think I'm going to try and do that. I figure it won't hurt to give you a call just to see how things are going. If I was dying I'd want you to call me that's for sure.

Anyway that's all I'm going to write for now. This notebook is filling up mad quick. When I finally get to Memphis I'll probably wind up telling you all of this anyway so what's the point of writing it all down right?

> *Love,*
> *Your Bro*

October 18thth, 2007

Dear Jamie,

Hi again. Did you get my card? It was just a simple piece of card stock with one of your Aunt Julie's watercolors on it. I think I sent it in a blue envelope with a stamp of the American flag.

I had been thinking about you and I just jotted a few things down about how things were in Cincinnati and my hopes that things were going well for you. I would be very sad if you decided to cut off communication with me. It would break my heart.

Would you please write me a quick note just to let me know how you're doing? And to be honest I would love to hear your voice. Will you give your worried mother a quick call?

I spoke with a woman at the academy infirmary and she assured me that you were still taking your medication and I was glad to hear that.

I realize this transition must be a difficult one. Please know your father and I and your brother Edward are thinking of you often and we're all looking forward to seeing you on Parents Weekend.

> *Love,*
> *Mom*

October 21st, 2007

Son,

You have exactly twenty-four hours upon receiving this letter to give your mother a call. She is beside herself with grief as to why you refuse to respond to her via a letter or the New Cadet pay phone. This has gone on for nearly a month and I will not tolerate your snobbishness.

As you know we will see you this weekend and I have faith that you will have had a conversation with her before our arrival at the academy.

I realize young men go through rough patches and can be confused by the world in a myriad of ways, but you are too intelligent, too informed in the ways of a gentleman, and we raised you too well to deserve such insolence. Do yourself a favor and call your mother.

Dad

March 12, 2008

Dear P,

It's been four days since I last wrote you. I've tried your phone number so many times P and it keeps saying it's been disconnected so I don't know what the deal is. And now I'm afraid to mail any of these letters to you. I guess I'll just keep them in this note-book till I know where you are because if your phone is disconnected then maybe that means you're not living in the same place too like maybe you moved into some special hospital and that really freaks me out because I'm trying to get to you!

I'm finally on Interstate 80 heading east. I'm eventually going to wind up on Interstate 55 going south to Memphis which is a pretty long ways but a lot has happened in the last few days and I need to tell you about it.

I spent another day with Lewis the she-man at the Lakeside Motel. He helped me do my laundry and let me use his shower again and fed me another microwave dinner and gave me forty dollars. He even offered to rent a car and drive me but I didn't have the guts to take him up on it because of his financial situation. I mean I know he's really broke and without a job and needs to start saving money so he can get that operation so he can have a dick. He gave me his phone number and said if I got into any trouble I should call him and he would come find me. Man that guy was cool P. Before I left he even showed me his chest. He was pretty shy about it but I really wanted to see it. He had just gotten out of the shower and he was wearing a T-shirt and I asked him if I could see it and he looked at me long and hard and then he took his shirt off and it really looked pretty good. I mean it wasn't like Brad Pitt's chest or anything but it looked like a man's chest and I couldn't tell that he ever had breasts.

He told me how the doctor had to remove his nipples first and then rebuild his chest and how they had to sew his nipples back on after that like they were the eyes of a teddy bear or something and then he sort of goofed around and flexed and we laughed and then he put his shirt back on.

A few hours later I packed my stuff and we said good-bye and I walked over to that big parking lot with all the truckers because I figured one of them might be heading south or east or maybe going in both directions.

It was a really nice day like seventy degrees and clear skies like you could see planes up there and these three truckers were playing horseshoes and this big black one named Luther saw me watching and invited me to play. He looked at me and said "I need a teammate" so I played and I did okay even though we lost to these two Native American Indian dudes who looked like father and son. Luther paid them twenty bucks each so I guess they were betting. I had a chance to tie the game with my last toss but I missed the stake. I said I was sorry but Luther was like "It ain't nothing" and told me not to worry about it. The truth is that I had that forty bucks Lewis the she-man gave me but I couldn't afford to lose any of it.

Luther wound up buying me a hamburger at that stand with the classic rock and this scratchy-voiced skeezer with sunburn cream on her nose served us. She was like "Hey Luther. What's the word?" and he said "The word is I might have to get a hip replaced. Goddamn forty-four years old walkin' around with titanium in me. Set off all the metal detectors. Everyone's gonna think I'm a terrorist." Then the hamburger lady said "Not you. Not my Luther."

Luther ate two hot dogs and I ate my burger even though Lewis had just fed me. Luther said "You got some appetite huh?" and I just nodded and kept my head down because I had no idea where the next free meal might come from.

Luther said he could get me as far south as Cheyenne but that's where he needed to head west on Interstate 80 and I was cool with that so he drove me like three hundred miles south. He had this whole mini-apartment set up in the back of his trailer with a bed and a flat-screen TV and a DVD player and a weight bench with a bunch of dumbbells and huge forty-five-pound plates stacked around it. Luther was like six six P no shit and mad ripped despite his hip problem. The only freaky thing about him was that he sort of smelled like piss and it made me wonder if he had some sort of disease and had to wear adult diapers or maybe he secretly LIKED to smell that way like he pissed his pants as much as possible. I got used to it after a while though just like anything else.

He couldn't stop talking about his wife who was back in Roanoke Virginia like how he couldn't wait to see her and how they had their ten-year anniversary coming up and how they liked to watch Pink Panther movies together. He was like "That Pink Panther dude is one funny cat."

I kept trying to imagine his wife and the person that kept coming into my head was that big fat black lady named Takada who used to come over and clean the kitchen when Mom's carpel tunnel syndrome was bad.

Anyway Luther was obsessed with his wife and even called her on his cell phone and said all this romantic stuff to her like "Yeah Sweetness you know I'm comin' home soon" and "I can't wait to see you too baby-girl."

I thought a lot about how his wife would deal with him smelling like piss like did she always have to Febreze him and how many pairs of pants had he ruined? But maybe his wife pissed her pants too and it was why they fell in love? Mysterious right?

He dropped me off at a Best Western in Lisco Nebraska which was cool because he wound up going about twenty miles east just to make sure I would be okay. The old skeezer behind the desk at the Best Western had a face like a mustard stain and kept talking about this place called Goblin Valley Utah. I had no idea why she was bringing up some weird place in Utah because I was in Nebraska!

She said "Unusual place that Goblin Valley" and I was like "Word."

I convinced her that my dad had dropped me off and would be by later to pay for the room. I told her he was a professional wrestler and his name was Valentin the Russian and that he has this move where he makes you eat the phone book. I have no idea why I made up that lie P but I think she believed me. I know I shouldn't mess with old people like that but at least it was a creative lie. She wound up giving me a room on the third floor with a balcony that looked out over the parking lot. I knocked a PayDay loose from the vending machine and after I ate it my stomach felt funny and then I got diarrhea again.

What was cool was that no one ever came to check on me and I wound up crashing at the Best Western for free I shit you not P. It was maybe my luckiest break since meeting Lewis the she-man at the Lakeside Motel.

I think maybe that old woman was senile like Grandma Beauty. Remember how if we stayed at her house in Louisville she would come down to the basement and say good-bye to us like four times and how she couldn't even remember that she had done it just a few minutes earlier and how Mom had to come down after like the third time and tell her that she had already said her good-byes? I think the old woman behind the desk had those kinds of brain-damage problems. I know there's a word for that kind of disease but I can't think of it right now. I keep wanting to say it's the Heimlich maneuver but I know that's where you get behind someone in like a butt-sex position and thrust them in the stomach with a fist ball when they're choking. This big dumb football player from my junior high named Chad Haggis used to do that to me even when I WASN'T choking. He'd be like "Heimlich maneuver!" and then he would chase me around and if he caught me he would put me in that position and start thrusting upwards with a fist ball till I would call him the Master of My Domain. "Say it!" he'd yell "Say it!" and I would say "You're the Master of My Domain Master Haggis!" and then he would have fake butt-sex with me for a bit and let me go.

In my free room at the Best Western I took a bubble bath for like an hour and got all the good stuff out of the minibar like the peanut M&M's and a can of Pringles and the bag of Cape Cod potato chips and two cans of Coke and I have to admit I took some liquor minis too. I got a Jim Beam and a Jack Daniel's and this small bottle of red wine that I probably won't be able to drink because I don't have a corkscrew but I figured maybe I could sell it or trade it with someone. It all fit in Sam's book bag pretty well. I wound up watching cable for a few hours and fell asleep with the TV on.

I had this crazy dream where I was in the motel room I was alone and it was the Best Western but there was no bed in the room. Instead there was this weird stainless steel manhole-type thing. It had a bubble-shaped top and when I walked up to it I could feel it sort of vibrating like crazy and when I reached down to touch it it started making all this noise like a train was coming or something and then all of a sudden the thing opened up and there was this freaky blue water kind of glowing all still and thickish and then out of nowhere that Scarlett Johansson skeezer came out of the water. She was naked and she took this huge gulp of air and her breasts looked MAD amazing but instead of nipples she had two little DAISIES and after she caught her breath she said "There's nowhere to go!" but I could have sworn it was Lewis the she-man's voice that came out of her mouth. I was like "You can stay here with me Hollywood Skeezer! There's no bed but we can make it work!" But she took a huge breath and dove back down into the water and then the stainless steel bubble-top thing closed and then I dropped to my knees and screamed "LET HER COME BACK PLEASE GOD OF THUNDER AND MERCY LET HER COME BACK!" And then when I looked down the daisies that were her nipples were on the floor and when I reached down to pick them up they turned into two giant Iraqi camel spiders and crawled up my leg!

I woke up with a jerk and I practically threw myself out of bed P I shit you not. It was really early in the morning maybe like six thirty which is really weird because that's what time reveille was at Buckner which makes me worried that there's some sort of permanent thing stuck in my brain now and that I'm going to start waking up at six thirty for the rest of my life. Maybe I can get hypnotized or something? Do you know anyone who can do that? Maybe I can learn how to meditate so that all that stuff that happened at Buckner will like empty out through some hidden drain in my ear?

Anyway I left my room key in the door and sneaked down the cement steps and across the parking lot and right by the window of the motel office. Some dude with a mustache was behind the desk now but he didn't see me so I just kept walking.

There was a twenty-four-hour restaurant next to the Best Western called The Country Kitchen. There were only a few people eating and one waitress who walked like she was squeezing a walnut between her ass cheeks and it sort of made me tense. I ordered pancakes and sausage patties from her and it took her forever to bring me my food and I was starting to get a little worried that that dude with the mustache at the Best Western was going to come over and make me pay for my room and look in my book bag at all the stuff I stole and call the cops or something.

Someone had scratched their name into the window at my booth. The name was CESAR and I thought if I ever changed my name that this might be a good choice. What do you think P? Have you ever thought about changing your name?

The window looked out at a Shell station and also out at the highway where cars were still driving with their lights on and I started to wonder what Branson was up to like did he miss me or was I just another Spanish Dave or Tom-Tom to him. I thought maybe I was and that made it easier to put Portland out of my mind.

The waitress came over and asked if I was sure I could pay for my food and she was holding it in front of me like I was a dog or something. I pulled my money out of my sock and put it right on the table and stared at her and she said "You know I'm gonna have to put rubber gloves on to take that from you" and I said "So do it." I really said that too P like I commanded it. I even felt my chest flexing and it felt good like I was a black belt in kung fu. She walked away from me muttering something under her breath.

When I was putting the money back in my sock this man came up to me and told me he loved my shoes. He was like "Cool shoes. I love New Balance." He had black curly hair with little slits for eyes and he had this weird half smile on his face like someone punched him when he was laughing and it got stuck that way. He asked me what I was doing and I said I was chilling and then he asked me if I was a model. I swear P he said "Are you a model?" and I said "No why?" and he went "You could be is all. You have that look."

I couldn't tell how old he was because he had one of those chubby faces and his lips were so small it was like they were drawn on with a pencil. Then he offered me a hundred bucks to go have my picture taken in his studio. He said "I'm a legit photographer I swear" and then he showed me a card with a website on it. It didn't have his name on it just the website.

I asked him if his studio was east or west of the restaurant and he said it was about thirty minutes east so I paid the check and got into his car with him and we drove east to some little town.

We didn't talk much in the car and he kept smiling his weird half smile. P I know when you read this you'll probably be like "J what the hell are you doing getting into a car with that weirdo!" but he seemed more normal than I'm making him out to be P he really did.

At one point I said "So are you like a professional photographer or something?" and he said he was trying to be and that him and his wife were starting up a portrait business and how they needed some samples to hang in their shop.

His studio was in the back of a locksmith's and when we walked in this big fat Chinese woman who was sitting behind a counter waved at him and he waved back and told me she was his wife and I said "Hey" to her and she waved at me too but she didn't say anything which made me think she was either deaf or couldn't speak English. The other weird thing about her was that she had this tube attached to her nose like some sort of medical tube but I couldn't see what it was connected to.

The smiling man led me to a back room which had this big gray backdrop thing and some pretty nice-looking camera equipment like the kind of stuff you could sell on eBay.

When he was setting up his camera he asked me my name and I told him it was Cesar and I'm sure the guy who etched it into the window at The Country Kitchen would be pissed if he knew I was pretending to be him without his permission. Then I asked him his name and he said it was Will Patterson and then he put this terrible music on and started taking pictures. I asked who it was and he said "Hootie and the Blowfish. You like it?" I said "Sure" even though I was lying. Then he said "Hootie's the best. Hootie and Counting Crows. I can't get enough of them either." He had to stop for a second and adjust this big light but he went right back to his camera and kept shooting.

He said "You're doing great Cesar just great."

I thought he was going to get all pervy and ask me to take my shirt off or make me like open my mouth so he could throw a grape in it or squirt water on me but all he did was ask me to hold a toy train engine. First I sat on a stool with the train in my lap and then I stood with the train and then I sat Indian-style on the floor with the train in my lap again. Once he put the train on the stool and adjusted my chin but that's the only time he touched me.

At one point he had to change film and that's when I put the rubber Halloween mask on. I sneaked it out of the book bag when he wasn't looking and then he looked up. He just stood there staring at me and I said "Go ahead. Take my picture" and he totally did it P I shit you not! In fact I think he took like FOURTEEN pictures because I counted. Eventually I took the mask off because I was getting mad hot and he never even asked me about it.

At the end of the shoot he really did give me a hundred bucks. They were all twenties and when we were about to get back in his car I asked him if he could drive me east instead of back to The Country Kitchen and he asked how far and I said whatever he could do and he was like "Okay. East then."

On the radio there was a commercial about herpes medication and then one about the Christian Church of the Fellowship and then one about Goodyear radial tires. His car smelled like foot odor and coleslaw and I hadn't noticed this when he drove me to the locksmith's.

On his steering wheel was a leather cover that had "Rich" on it. I said "I thought your name was Will" and he said it was Will and then I asked him why it said Rich on his steering wheel and he said "That's not a name that's a goal."

He wound up driving me about thirty more miles east and dropped me off at a rest stop on Interstate 80 somewhere near this place called Ogallala. We shook hands like we were old friends even though I knew that was bullshit but I was genuinely amped about the cash he paid me.

Before he got back in his car he told me I was a great model and I had this urge to ask him why his wife had those tubes in her nose but I didn't. For some reason I can't get that out of my head P.

When his car pulled out of the rest stop I felt like I had escaped something terrible. I guess Will could have done all sorts of weird shit to me like he could have even murdered me and cut me up into a thousand pieces and like MAILED them all over the country but all he wanted was to take my picture so he could have some samples for his business. That's not so bad right? He's probably a really nice person.

At the rest stop I found an atlas that someone had left on a picnic table and I opened it up to where I was. I had to get all the way across Nebraska and then Iowa and then Illinois and then Kentucky! That's a lot of states P! I had no idea how big this country is. It's mad huger than any other country I'm sure. I mean I've seen maps in school and I remember thinking Canada was big but I think maybe America is bigger.

The good news is that I have a hundred and forty bucks in my pocket now so if I can get to a train station I can stop hitchhiking and somehow get to Memphis.

So it's pretty nice at this rest stop. There's a picnic table in the grass and I'm eating Cape Cod potato chips and drinking a can of Coke. P I have to admit that I just poured my Jim Beam mini into my Coke. There's nothing like a joke Coke to even the day out. Don't worry I made sure no cops were around. This van pulled in a few minutes ago and this guy with a Chicago White Sox hat got out and stretched and did some squats next to his van and then got back in and drove away.

So I've been getting a little drunk and I'm feeling pretty good P. I'm "tight" as Branson would say.

I tried calling you again. I called you collect from the public pay phone but like before it says your phone has been disconnected. I don't understand that P. Have you already died? Is that how you know when someone dies for sure? The morgue has some special deal with the phone company and they punch in a code and disconnect you?

I'm not going to get too mad at you because you're sick and there could be a thousand reasons why your phone's been disconnected.

I've been thinking about starting to walk east on Interstate 80. It's a stupid thought I know because a cop would definitely stop me but I'm on my second joke Coke and I'm liable to do anything.

I think I need to go lie in the grass.

Love,
Your Bro

November 6th, 2007

Dear Jamie,

Hi. Thanks for your letter. My mom just got me a new MacBook with the Leopard system, which I like a lot. In fact, I'm writing this very letter to you on it!

I had no idea you had gone away to that school until your brother told me. A military academy sounds like a very intense place. I know your father was in the army so it must run in the family. I'm not sure I could handle military school. I can barely handle regular public school, although I am doing better than I did in eighth grade. After I got in trouble this past summer for partying with those German exchange students I read this book called *Jonathan Livingston Seagull* and it made me really want to change my life. Have you heard of it? You should read it, Jamie, you really should.

I'm very flattered by your invitation to go to the Midwinter Ball but I have to decline because I'm seeing someone and I already promised him that I would be his date to the Snow Ball here in Cincinnati. But the Midwinter Ball sounds fun. I have never been to a military academy formal before and I'm sure having the girls stay on campus for a night must be exciting for the cadets. I can't imagine going to boarding school. I can barely imagine going away to college at this point.

By the way, I should tell you that the person I started dating is your brother Edward. I know it must be weird for you to hear that because of your invitation and because of the fact that he's a senior and I'm a freshman, but it's not as strange as it sounds. He may not have told you because he didn't want to hurt your feelings, but it's true. He's very intense and straightlaced, but I think that's good for me as I'm not smoking anymore and I've given up alcohol and pot, too. And my parents really like him and think he's impressive.

Anyway, Jamie, I've missed seeing you on the block but I'm sure I'll see you when you get your military holidays. By the way, did you hear that the Fergusons were on the Jay Leno show? They were in the audience and the camera landed right on them. Ben Affleck was Jay's guest. How lucky are the Fergusons?!

Best of luck at your school and if I can think of anyone who might want to be your date to the Midwinter Ball I'll let you know.

Sincerely,
Cornelia Zenkich

BUCKNER MILITARY ACADEMY
2700 OLD CEMETERY ROAD
REVERE, MO 63465

OFFICIAL MEMORANDUM

DATE: 24 OCTOBER 2007

TO: CADET RECRUIT WYCKOFF

FROM: THE COMMANDANT'S OFFICE

YOUR PRESENCE IS REQUESTED AT COLONEL
STOOPS' OFFICE TOMORROW, THURSDAY,
OCTOBER 25, 2007, AT 1600 HOURS.

PLEASE BE PREPARED TO DISCUSS YOUR
RECENT FAILINGS AT MONDAY DRILL.

COLONEL STOOPS HAS REQUESTED THAT
YOU BRING YOUR GYM CLOTHES AS WELL AS
YOUR M.T.-I TRAINING MANUAL. HE WILL BE
PROVIDING A WORLD WAR I WINCHESTER
DRILL RIFLE.

September18th, 2007

Dearest James,

Just a quick note to say hello and that I hope you enjoy the care package. I know your mother isn't too keen on you eating sweets, but I took the liberty of adding a few things I thought you might enjoy. The brownies are homemade, my own special recipe in fact. And I know your birthday isn't until mid-March, but I thought I would include a little money to keep in your pocket.

Louisville is enjoying an unseasonably warm fall. The leaves have yet to change but I have faith. The other night I took in a Shakespeare play at Actor's Theater. I think it was supposed to be *Measure for Measure* but I have no idea what the director and his sub-par cast were trying to communicate. There was a young man in the cast who looked like your brother Peter but that's about the only joy I left the theater with.

I understand that you will be attending a non-denominational Wednesday chapel service as well as a mass on Sunday mornings at which you will be able to take communion. I hope you will keep your

Catholic faith in mind and all that Christ suffered on our behalf.

I very much look forward to seeing you at Thanksgiving again. I plan on driving up with your Aunt Julie in my old jalopy, should it make it to Cincinnati.

Best of luck with everything, James. I love you very much.

God Bless You and Keep You,
Grandma Beauty

March 15th, 2008

Dear P,

So it's three days later.

P life is really weird really really weird but I'm sure you already know that.

The days and the nights and animals talking to you in your dreams and the way people smell and faces that remind you of other faces and seven-foot giants walking around at the Taco Bell and how many burritos they have to eat to get full and things getting invented in basements and the war still going on in the Middle East and what it must feel like to kill a person and some guy in Venice California jumping over a building on his skateboard and what happens to fish during a tidal wave and how some people are born with huge brown moles on their backs and why can't I get any pubic hair and who makes up all those tests you have to take where you fill in the little ovals and what did the Native American Indians think when they started building all the highways and some woman giving birth to a goldfish in Florida and how do you wake up one day and decide you want to be an astronaut?

I mean these are serious problems P! Serious serious problems and issues and they make me feel like I'm on meth again even though I am definitely not. Meth is about the last thing I want to be on right now but I do wish I had some of my medication because I'm having trouble focusing P focusing on anything right now is hard so I decided to write you again because it's the only thing that makes me feel better.

What happened since I last wrote you is this Chrysler LeBaron pulled into the rest stop. It was red with a beige convertible top and the moment I saw it I knew it would be important in my life. Has that ever happened to you P? I've heard about how someone will find a dog or see a cloud making some weird shape or discover something random written on a napkin like REMEMBER WHERE YOU LEFT YOUR HEAD and you know it will be like a part of your destiny. That's sort of what it was like when I saw the LeBaron. It was the first time I've ever had that feeling P sort of like when I ice-skated with E for the first time on Duck Lake in Michigan or when I did my first legit headfirst dive off the high dive or my first bong hit in seventh grade with this big tall kid Rabbit Cleveland whose parents were professional hippies and lived half the year in a Winnebago. The LeBaron was sort of like all of that but more intense I shit you not.

Anyway this man got out of the car. There was nothing particularly special about him. He was tall and needed a shave and maybe he was even a little tan but in a natural way. He was sort of old and young at the same time like maybe as old as the Major but maybe a little younger it was hard to tell. He didn't have one of those potbellies that older dudes get and his hair was sort of long and gray but in a cool way like it was almost silver. I got the sense that he'd been around like maybe he had one of those ancient souls you sometimes hear about. He wore jeans and a beat-up plain black T-shirt and a pair of Chuck Taylors.

He put the hood up and started checking his oil when I walked over to him. I said "Hey" and he looked at me over his shoulder and said "Hey what?" and I was like "You drivin' east?" and he said he was heading east and I told him how I was trying to get to Memphis and he said "Memphis huh?" and I nodded and he said "That's not just east. You gotta go south too." I said I know and then he asked me if I was in some sort of a jam and I said I wasn't and he was like "If I take you to Memphis what do I get out of it?" and I told him I had money and then he finally turned completely around and looked at me. He was holding a rag that was stained with motor oil. He was taller than I thought too even taller than you P which is tall.

He said "How am I supposed to know you're not some sorta serial killer?" I told him I wasn't and he said "You never know about that type of thing." I went "I've never killed anyone" and then he put the rag down and said "You been drinkin'?" and I said "Maybe" and he said "Sure smells that way" so I told him that I'd had a few and he was like "You're a little young for that don't you think?" and I went "Are you like my dad or something?" and he said "Not that I know of. You tryin to tell me I should take a blood test?" and I said "No" and he was like "Well that's a relief" and then he asked me my age and I told him fifteen even though technically speaking I wasn't yet and he said "Just what I need. An underage drunk on my hands" and I was like "I'm not a drunk" and he said "What are you then a beverage consultant?" Then he dropped the hood on the LeBaron and said "Memphis is pretty far. I was planning on heading due east" and I told him if he could get me to Interstate 55 that I could get south on my own which was true P because I had figured it all out with that atlas.

Then I offered him a hundred and forty bucks and he said "That's a lot of money. You could open a taco stand with that kinda cash. You ever think about opening a taco stand?" I said "No" and then he asked me if I liked tacos and I said that sometimes I did and then he sort of sized me up but not in a creepy way and said "You just got that backpack?" and I nodded and then he told me to get in and said "But if you murder me I'm gonna have to kick your ass. Deal?" and I nodded and got in his car.

The inside of the LeBaron smelled like lighter fluid and peppermint. He listened to classic rock and rolled down the window to smoke Pall Malls which I've heard are like the most powerful cigarettes ever created and it made me want to smoke so bad it was like there was a cat clawing out the inside of my stomach. He had this brass Zippo lighter that he flicked at a lot but besides the radio and the sound of the LeBaron that was pretty much the only noise for a long time. We hardly talked for a hundred miles P but for some reason I wasn't tense. I just looked out the window and sort of thought about the past few days and all the weird shit that had happened. I had this sad feeling when I thought about Lewis the she-man and for some reason that made me think about you and how you're dying and I almost lost my shit but I didn't because I kept digging the nail of my index finger into the knuckle of my thumb and now I have this total red mark there.

I knew things would be cool when he gave me a cigarette. He offered it without asking. P I know you don't smoke but I think smokers have superpowers when it comes to other smokers. When he lit me he said "Now don't go gettin' lung cancer on account of this."

After I finished the cigarette I almost asked him for another one but I didn't want to push my luck. I could tell he was one of those guys who doesn't like a mooch.

About ten minutes later he said "You smoke like you know what you're doin'" and I said "I know how to smoke" and he was like "Drinkin' smokin'. What else you got up your sleeve? You know how to play poker?" I said "No" and he said "You a black belt in karate?" and I was like "I wish" which is true P because if I was a black belt or I had world-class equivalence like Fat Larkin I probably wouldn't have gotten jumped because my senses would have been mad honed and I would have known those dudes were behind me in the bathroom with that forty of Bud.

We got off the highway near this town called Gothenburg and he asked me if I was hungry and I was pretty starved even though the cigarette definitely helped calm my stomach. There was a Wendy's just off the exit and as we were pulling into the parking lot he said "So much for watching my cholesterol" and then he asked me my name and I told him and asked him his and he said it was Kent and then he asked if I minded if we hit the drive-through because he said he was on a tight schedule and I said I didn't mind at all. Man I was acting polite P and I have no idea why. Maybe it was because he was so cool.

I ordered exactly what he did which was a single with cheese and a small Frosty. Kent got a salad too.

After he put our order through he rolled up the window and said "No roughage huh?" and I said "I don't roll like that" and he was like "You don't ROLL like that?" Then I told him salad was for old people and he said "Tell that to your colon when you hit about thirty-seven."

While we were eating this song called "Gimme Shelter" by The Rolling Stones came on the radio. I've never been much of a Stones fan P but it sounded really good in the LeBaron. I think Kent had one of those high-end German systems called Blaupunkt that Fat Larkin used to talk about all the time. While we ate Kent sort of sang along to The Stones under his breath. I asked him if he liked The Stones and he said they were the best. He said he liked the Beatles too and then we didn't speak for a while.

Nebraska was really flat. There were like a hundred miles of fields on both sides. Fields with silos and farmhouses and big red rickety barns that seemed like they were leaning away from bad news. I thought Missouri was boring but Nebraska was like looking at some stupid painting of the land for three hours.

I was about to fall asleep when Kent said "So what's in Memphis anyway?" I told him you were there and he asked me if you were older or younger than me and I told him how you're twenty-seven and I told him how Mom and the Major and E were in Cincinnati but how I'd been hanging out in Portland for the past six months. Kent sort of nodded and then he didn't ask anymore questions. He didn't give me the third degree about why I was hitchhiking or how come I wasn't in school.

By the time we got to Iowa Kent and I were getting along pretty well. We stopped for dinner at a Ponderosa outside of Des Moines and that's when he asked me if I wanted to keep traveling with him. He said "So you sobered up yet?" and I told him I was cool and then he asked me why I drank and if I was bored with life and I said maybe a little and then he said he could turn me in so I asked him if he was a cop anyway and he went "A COP?" and sort of grunted.

After the waitress brought us waters I asked him if he drank alcohol and he said "You're damn right I do but I'm allowed to" and then he ordered a steak with a baked potato so I did too.

I was totally biting his style P which is something I learned from Branson. If you copied him in any way he would be like "Stop bitin' my style Zilla. Stop BITIN'!" Once I started wearing one sock pushed down on my left ankle because he was doing it and he stopped me from walking out of our room and made me pull it back up and called me a biting-ass bitch so I've tried not to bite anyone's style since but I sort of couldn't help it with Kent.

After we ordered Kent pulled out a cell phone and made a call. He had an old ghetto BlackBerry like the kind with the wheel on the side. I think he called some skeezer because the first thing he said was "Hey Angel." I tried to be polite and not listen. The conversation didn't last very long and I distracted myself by watching the waitress talk to the cook. She was pretty young maybe like a college student and she had a decent face but she couldn't stand still for more than three seconds and I thought that that would drive me crazy if she was my girl. I mean I'm nervous enough about shit especially lately and not being on my medication probably doesn't help. The last thing I need is a skeezer with the heebie-jeebies.

After Kent put his BlackBerry away he asked me if I liked being his travel partner and I told him it was okay and he said "It's just okay?" so I admitted I liked it and then he asked me if I wanted to continue on with him through the rest of Iowa and Illinois. He even said that if things went well he might be able to get me all the way to Memphis. I told him I would pay him but he said I didn't have to and then I asked him what he wanted in exchange for it and he said "Just be my partner. Watch my back" and

I said okay and then he said "But no drinkin'" and I nodded and then he said "Unless I'm doin' it" and we both laughed. It was the first time I had smiled in a while and it made my face feel really weird and tired.

The next day he got a shave and a haircut at a barbershop in this town called Grinnell and he offered to pay for a haircut for me too. I was like "You think I need a haircut?" and he said "You LIKE lookin' like that?" and I went "Lookin' like what?" I thought he was going to say "Like a girl" but he didn't instead he said "Like a punk" and then I said "But I am a punk" and I told him how in Portland they called me Punkzilla but he was like "You're not in Portland anymore" so I got my hair cut really short like sort of a shaggy crew cut and now I'm blond again.

When I was walking back to the LeBaron Kent said "There he is" and I liked when he said that P I have to admit that I liked it a lot.

That night we stayed in a motel in eastern Iowa. I was so tired I fell asleep in the car and woke up while he was carrying me into our room. I looked up at him and he said "Just go to sleep" and I nodded and woke up the next morning in the opposite bed with my clothes on. He had taken my New Balances off and placed them at the foot of the bed.

The best was the shower. I stayed in there for like a half hour. I used the motel soap and shampoo and Kent got me a toothbrush and some toothpaste. He told me to make sure to brush my teeth and that he didn't want a travel partner with dog breath so I brushed the shit out of my teeth and looked at myself in the mirror at my short blond hair and then I checked to see if I had gotten my first pube but I hadn't.

That morning we drove across the Mississippi River into Illinois. I had no idea how big that river is P. You could see these boats in the distance. They looked like big floating birthday cakes. Man that area of the country seemed really old-fashioned like maybe they didn't know about the Internet or like at any moment someone was going to start playing a banjo or something but I have to admit that I liked that feeling P. At least looking out on the Mississippi I did.

As we were going over the bridge Kent said "So what do your parents do besides put up with you?" and I told him how the Major's a retired Major in the army and how Mom is basically just a mom.

He said "Being just a mom can be rough business" and I told him how she's depressed and how I worry about her and he asked if I talked to her much and I said not lately and he suggested I give her a call and said I could use his cell phone so I took his ghetto BlackBerry and called home and after a few rings Mom answered. She was like "Hello?" but I couldn't say anything. She said "Hello?" again and I felt like all the blood was leaving my stomach. I swallowed as hard as I could and then hung up and gave Kent his BlackBerry back. He said "No luck?" and I shook my head and then he asked me about the Major like if I got along with him and I said not really and then I told him how I got sent to Buckner and he asked me what I did to deserve that and I told him I basically screwed around too much and he was like "I gather you didn't care for all the military stuff" and I said I didn't and he said he didn't blame me which was cool and then I asked him if he was ever in the military and he told me about how he got drafted for Vietnam but how he went up to Canada to hide and how he spent twelve years up there and then I asked him how old he was and he said "Older than you think" and I said "What are you like sixty-something?" and he said "I'm like for me to know and you to find out how about that?" and then he told me about how when he was my age he lived in Burlington Wisconsin and how his parents moved around a lot and how his dad was a tool-and-dye man and how his family had to go wherever his dad could get work and how he went to the first half of high school in Vermont and the other half in Clearwater Florida and how before he went up to Canada he'd spent a few years on a fishing boat up in Alaska.

Then I asked him if he had any brothers or sisters and he said he had a sister Rita who had died five years ago from a stroke and then I asked him what he did for money and he said he mostly painted houses and drove around the country like he would drive peoples' cars across the United States but he said the LeBaron was his and that he was on a thinking vacation.

And then I asked him if he was married and he said he was but that she left him for some rich bastard and how the rich bastard left her for some teenager with big blue eyes. His ex-wife's name was Marty which he said is short for Martina. Then he said they were planning on meeting up later and I was like "Word" and I was really looking forward to meeting her too P because I figured anyone he was involved with must be mad cool.

While the radio station played a rock block of The Clash Kent looked over and asked me how my new haircut was treating me and I told him I liked it. After that most of Illinois was a blur like tons more fields and all these cows sort of standing around like men talking about money or something. The weird thing about cows P is that when it's about to rain they huddle like they're playing FOOTBALL or something! I was like "What are they doing?" and Kent said "Makin' plans. They'll prolly take over this godforsaken world at some point. The cows and the goats and all the other things we pump the hormones into. I'd trust them more than that fool who's running things now" and he totally meant President Bush P. See you would have loved this guy!

It rained for a while and I fell asleep sort of using the seat belt as a pillow and then we stopped to get gas in this little town on Route 31 called Geneva. We wound up staying in this little place called the Geneva Motel that was run by this married couple that looked like they just got out of the hospital.

There were a bunch of Winnebagos in the parking lot and I thought it was weird how those people
had a place to sleep in their Winnebagos but chose to
stay in a motel. I figured their toilets were jacked up
or something.

Our room had two queen beds and cable and a
kitchenette with a microwave oven and a coffeemaker.

Later Kent's ex-wife Marty came and met us
for dinner. We went to this place called Isabella's
that had white tablecloths and mood music. Earlier when I was taking a nap Kent bought me a shirt
with a collar and a pair of brown leather shoes. The
shirt was blue with little buttons to keep the collar
down. Mom would love this shirt P. Kent bought
me a pair of pants too and the weird thing is that
everything he got me fit perfectly like EXACTLY
perfectly!

He put a shirt with a collar on too and a pair of
dark blue pants and we headed to the restaurant.

When we got in the LeBaron he asked me if I
liked swordfish and I told him I'd never had it but
that's what I ordered and it was mad tasty. Kent
ordered the lamb chops and Marty ate some grilled
vegetables. Marty was really tall and pretty with long
brown hair and big brown eyes. Even though she was

hot for her age she sort of had a sad look on her face like nothing worked out right in her life.

When Kent introduced us he said "Marty this is my partner in crime Jamie. Jamie meet Marty the woman who broke my heart."

I put my hand out for her to shake and she took it and then she sort of bent down and kissed me on the cheek. She might have been six feet tall P I shit you not and I could tell she was a classy woman with nice manners.

And I have to tell you this P because I would be lying if I didn't. What happened was that when Marty kissed me on the cheek I got a boner and I had to sit with my legs crossed for like twenty minutes. I didn't dare get up to use the bathroom or anything.

They ordered a bottle of red wine and drank most of it. Man I wanted some even though I'm not no wino. Branson used to drink this stuff once in a while called Zima but that was some other kind of wine like it has 7-Up and baking soda in it or something.

During dinner you could tell how Marty was still in love with Kent because he could make her laugh any time he wanted just by looking at her in a certain way.

Things got sort of serious when Kent said "So whose heart are you breakin' these days?" Marty said there was no one in her life and Kent was like "You mean they're not beating down your door like they used to?" and she said they weren't and then he told her she was prettier than ever. He was like "You're prettier than ever Marty. I'm right ain't I kid?" To Marty I said "Yeah you're pretty" and she smiled and asked me how I fit into Kent's life but before I could answer Kent said "Me and the boy go way back don't we?" and I nodded and looked at Marty who was looking back at me with tears in her eyes and I started feeling tense for some reason. Then Marty said she was glad we found each other but it came out funny almost like she was jealous or something. P I had no idea what the fuck was going on.

After we paid the check Kent gave me the keys to the LeBaron and walked Marty to her car and they had a long kiss and she totally like clung to him for a long time like when you throw a cat end-over-end into some curtains but Kent eventually pushed her off him and she got in her car and he shut her door for her.

She drove a Mercedes P I shit you not like one

of those really nice 380SLs. It was white and really clean.

When Kent came back to the LeBaron he asked me if I wanted to drive and I told him I didn't know how but he said he would teach me. I was like "What if we get caught?" and he said "What if what if what if. Too many what ifs will drive a man to church every Sunday."

He had me sit in front of the wheel and powered the seat up so I could see over the dashboard and told me about the accelerator and the brakes and told me the only way I was going to learn to drive right was by doing it and it was starting to get dark out so he turned the headlights on and I drove around the parking lot of the restaurant a few times and he totally showed me how to use the turn signal and the rearview mirror and the side mirror and made me test the brakes so I would know how hard I'd have to press down on them to make them work right. I was a nervous wreck P. I think my hands were shaking worse than the morning after I did that meth with Branson. I was trying hard to not be a pussy I really was.

Just before I pulled out onto the main road this old man and his wife looked into the car. They were dressed up like they were about to go golfing. I think they were pretty freaked out because of how young I looked. Kent rolled the window down and told them he was teaching his son how to drive and the old man went "Go get 'em Slim!" and then he and his wife both smiled and all of their false teeth sort of flashed white.

Then I drove back to the Geneva Motel P I shit you not. It was one of the coolest feelings. I mean I know everyone learns how to drive at some point but I had no idea how awesome it is. The LeBaron was totally under my control. Branson would've been so amped and jealous at the same time!

I imagine that you're not driving so much these days P but you probably have to once in a while right to like get your cancer medicine from the pharmacy? Or maybe Jorge takes you? What's cool is that now I can go get your medicine if you need me to P. I'll totally do it it's not a problem.

The drive back to the Geneva Motel was slow going I'll admit it. I had to really concentrate to not drift too close to the centerline. At one point Kent said "If you go any slower you're liable to get pulled over" so I jacked it up to the speed limit and man my balls felt mad huge! On the radio some Zeppelin song was playing and even though I didn't know the words I felt like I did. It even seemed like they wrote the song for ME.

The next day Marty picked me up at the motel and took me to this weird amusement park in East Dundee Illinois called Santa's Village. I was a little confused that Kent wasn't in the room when I woke up but Marty said he would meet us later. She wore a green dress and sandals and she smelled good. I asked her what kind of perfume she used and she said it was called Vivian Westwood and that they didn't make it anymore and that she only wore it on special occasions. Then she asked me if I liked it and I told her it smelled French and she looked at me and said there was cinnamon and orange blossom in it.

What was weird P was that it sort of felt like I was going on a DATE with Marty and she's like at least forty-something and really pretty and way out of my league. I mean she was all dressed up with lipstick and that fancy perfume.

In her Mercedes she was quiet for a while and then sort of out of nowhere she asked if Kent was my dad. She said "So is Kent your daddy?" and I was like "Did he tell you that?" and she said no but that she had this feeling that Kent and me had a secret. I said "We don't have a secret" and she said we were cut from the same cloth and that we even had the same color eyes and I was like "We do? What color are they?" and she said they were hazel and I went "I don't have hazel eyes" because I don't P. Mom always told me they were blue and then Marty asked me if I had looked in the mirror lately and I told her I looked in the mirror all the time and she said "You got the biggest hazel eyes I think I've ever seen" and then I told her that Kent and I didn't have a secret again and she got all weird and sad for like ten minutes.

Then I asked her if she and Kent were married even though I knew they had been and she said they were married for ten years and I asked her if it was good and she went "For a while it was. But then again no one is ever completely happy in a marriage." I asked her if they had kids and she said they almost did but they lost it and I said "Like at the grocery store?" and she said no that it died right after it was born and man that was shocking to hear P. Mad shocking. She said it only lived for a few hours and that it was a little boy and then I told her I was sorry and then she turned the radio on to an easy-listening station but this sad song was playing. It was this song about a house not being a home and a chair not being a chair so she turned it off and put some big-ass sunglasses on.

After a few more miles I said "Kent said you left him for some rich dude" and she sort of scoffed and laughed and I was like "That's not true?" and she said "He was more than just SOME RICH DUDE" and she went on to say how he also happened to be a wonderful person and I asked what his name was and she said Ben and she also said that Kent had an interesting way of cheapening things. Then I asked her if she regretted leaving Kent and she said she did and that sometimes people make mistakes but that she was never really sure if he was up for a serious commitment and how at heart Kent's a journeyman and an adventurer and how most of the time when he's with you his head is somewhere else. Then she said "He'll wind up disappointing you too you'll see."

That really pissed me off when she said that P but I didn't say anything because of all that stuff about her son dying.

Then she asked me if I had a girlfriend and I said no and she said not to worry that I would and I was like "I doubt it" and she asked me if I liked boys and I said "I don't like boys!" and she said "It's okay if you do" and I went "I totally like skeezers." Then she told me I was a cutie and that I needed to give it some time and that I'd definitely break a few hearts before it was all over.

She adjusted her sunglasses and I could see how she was crying because a tear sort of fell down her cheek.

Then I asked her if she was still married to Ben even though I knew she wasn't. I guess I wanted to see what she would say and she said that she wasn't married to him anymore and I asked her why and she said because he left her and I asked her why again and she said this P she said "Because he didn't find me compelling anymore" and I said "Does that mean pretty?" and she said "I suppose it could" and then I told her I thought she was compelling and she said thank you and then she held her breath for a second and said "The woman Ben is with now is very young and beautiful."

Before I got out of the car I flipped the driver's side visor down and checked out my eyes and with my new haircut they did seem more hazel than blue. I could see what she was talking about in terms of how they were like Kent's and I wondered if he'd noticed this too.

We walked around Santa's Village for a while

and I think she was trying to pretend she was my mom or something because she kept holding my hand. There weren't too many people there and that made it feel like something bad had gone down like a kid had an epileptic fit on the roller coaster or some killer bees attacked a group of fifth-graders. Marty bought me some cotton candy and it was weird P. She was treating me like I was seven or eight.

When it got sort of hot and sunny she took out this sunblock stuff and put it all over her arms and face. She went "Here" and put some on my neck and told me I was fair.

Her hand felt pretty good on me P. I couldn't believe what I was thinking but I really had this weird urge to squeeze her breasts I really did! I would have been like "Hey Martina hook a brother up" but she was on some other trip with me and it was mad confusing.

After she finished with the sunblock she kissed me on the cheek and then she asked me for a hug so I walked into her arms. I actually tried to walk right into her BREASTS and she pulled me close and smelled my hair.

Then she said "Hey Mr. Magoo" and kissed the top of my head again and I said "Hey" back to her and she was like "Can you smell the orange blossom?" and I said I could and it was true P it was like a thousand orange blossoms were all around us and if there was any real chance of me putting my testicles on her breasticles that was it but I couldn't do it.

After the hug we went to the petting zoo and I wound up staring at this thing that looked like a cross between a sheep and a giraffe for like ten minutes. It had a face like it knew all sorts of shit about people and it seemed bored at the same time. I think it might have been a llama or some sort of desert camel. Marty said "Go ahead kiddo he's not going to bite" and that's when I turned to her and asked her where Kent was. I think it was the "kiddo" that pissed me off. She said he would be there soon so I just stared at the llama thing and it stared back at me.

After the petting zoo Marty pulled out a digital camera and took a bunch of pictures of me standing under this huge statue of Santa. After like the ninth one she said "Smile for this one" because I wasn't smiling for shit so I smiled but I thought I was going to be sick.

At one point she stopped this man who worked there and asked him to take our picture together and she went to a knee and hugged me around the waist.

After the pictures I asked her if we could go back to the motel. I told her I wasn't feeling good and that I thought I was going to puke in my mouth so she pulled out her cell phone and left Kent a message and then we left Santa's Village and headed back to the Geneva Motel.

About halfway there she reached over and sort of petted my head. Her hand stopped at the lump where I got hit with the forty. She asked what it was from and I lied and told her I fell down and hit the corner of a table and she said "Poor thing" and sort of stroked it for a second and then I jerked away and she asked what was wrong and I said nothing was wrong and then she said I seemed funny and then I was like "You don't even know me" and she said "But I'm enjoying GETTING to know you" and then I finally said it P I said "I'm not your son!" and man it was such a relief to say that.

After it was quiet she said "I'm sorry if I've made you feel uncomfortable" and I was like "Just take me back to Kent and hurry the fuck up" and then she got pissed and said "There's no need to swear" and I told her I'd swear if I wanted to and she started getting more pissed and said "Kent's not who you think he is. He runs from everybody and everything" and I said

"You left HIM you fucking skanky bitch" and then she stopped the car and slapped me across the face. I'm glad I had the seat belt on or I would have went through the windshield P. The tires really screeched to a halt like in the movies.

The slap stung pretty bad so I punched her in the right breast. I punched her hard too P. She even started crying and her mouth got really ugly and she told me to get out so I started to undo my seat belt.

She said "I won't have some punk kid calling me names and attacking me in my own car!" Then I said "Fuck you" pretty loud and slammed the door and started to walk away down this busy street.

Marty drove off pretty fast and I was glad I was out of her car. I mean it was a really nice Mercedes it was all leather on the inside and I'll probably never ride in one of those again but that skeezer was fucking crazy.

I wound up getting directions back to the Geneva Motel from this guy at a Marathon station. It was only a fifteen-minute walk and when I got back Kent wasn't there so I sat down in front of our door and fell asleep and had this dream that you were swimming P. You and I were in this public pool together and we were the only ones there and I had a swimsuit on but you were wearing all these clothes like sweaters and scarves and brown corduroy pants and you were having a really hard time so I kept saying "Tread water bro. Just keep treading water." You were laughing and making these dolphin noises. It was pretty funny but there was an ache in my chest.

I woke to Kent shaking my shoulder. I was like "Where were you?" He said he had some business to take care of and that he was on his way to Santa's Village when he got the call from Marty. He said "I understand you two got in a fight" but I didn't say anything. I just sat there.

Kent said "She's not right in the head."

When we got inside he told me how after they lost the baby she had to go into this hospital for mental illness for six months and how they never got back on track after that.

I asked him where he was and he said he went to go see Marty's mother who lives at an old-folks home that was about ten minutes away. He said they were pretty close and that she wasn't doing so hot and how Marty doesn't speak to her anymore and how he likes to drop in and say hello when he's passing through town. Then he said "We better hit the road huh?" I nodded and went to the bathroom while Kent paid the bill at the motel office.

Back in the LeBaron Marty called Kent's cell phone and asked to speak to me and I told him I didn't want to talk to her and he told her that and he also told her that I was stubborn and then he listened to her for a minute and turned to me and said "She's begging" and offered the phone so I took it.

I was like "What?" and she said she was sorry for kicking me out of her car. I said "Okay" and then she said she was sorry she slapped me and that she wasn't a bad person and I said "Okay" again and then she said "Please don't hate me" and I said "I don't" even though I pretty much did. Then I handed the phone back to Kent and he said good-bye to her and hung up and thanked me for talking to her and said that now she'll be able to sleep at night.

We drove for a while and listened to a Cubs game and Kent asked me if I played baseball and I told him I wasn't good at sports and I asked him if he played and he said he did when he was a kid but that when he got older he could never hit a curve ball.

In Joliet Illinois Kent brought this girl over to the Holiday Inn. She was really pale and had these light blue eyes and long wavy blond hair like the kind of hair you would want to paint if you were a painter but something seemed wrong with her like she moved slow or she was in pain. Kent called her Al but her name was Albertina and she wore a jean skirt and a PJ Harvey concert shirt. Remember how you used to listen to that PJ Harvey album Dry all the time P? Pretty cool right?

At first I couldn't tell what her and Kent's relationship was because Albertina kept sitting in his lap and hugging him around the neck.

"Hey Al" Kent kept saying. "Hey there now."

He was mad crazy about her P like his whole face lit up when they looked at each other.

Later she said "Mom tried to e-mail you" and that's when it was obvious that she was his daughter. He said "I never check that thing" and she said "I know. You owe me about fifty e-mails."

Then Kent pulled out a gold necklace with a locket and gave it to her and said "You like it?" and she smiled and said "Uh-huh" and turned it under the hotel lamp for a minute and then she put it on while he held her hair up. I watched her really hard P. She almost started crying she was so happy. Kent obviously meant a lot to her.

Kent said "Put a picture of your sweetheart in

it" but she was like "I don't have a sweetheart" and he said "What about that soccer player kid?" and she said that he was in love with his soccer ball and that that was boring.

Albertina was fourteen and was about to finish her freshman year at Joliet West High School. Kent couldn't stop talking about how she was a straight-A student.

"I got some Bs this year" she said. "Trig kicked my ass."

I have to admit that I was impressed P. It turns out that she also plays the cello and was about to travel to Springfield Illinois to audition for this special symphony for the exquisitely gifted but she has this thing called lupus that totally fucks with your joints and she was in the middle of what she called a flare-up.

"Was it bad this time?" Kent asked and she said "It got bad yeah" and she started telling him how she'd been having a really hard time getting out of bed.

"I have lupus" she told me right after that. "It's messing my heart up too." I just nodded and looked down.

Then Kent asked her how her hands were and

she said they were good and that lately it was her knees and hips that were aching the most.

We ordered a pepperoni pizza from this place called Happy Joe's and Kent went and got Cokes from down the hall. It was the first time me and Albertina were alone in the room. I asked her if she liked PJ Harvey and she said that she liked her old stuff mostly and that Uh Huh Her was pretty good too and then I tried not looking at her for a minute because she was starting to mad own my gaze like in a magnetic way and I didn't want to sweat her too much.

She asked me how I knew her dad and I told her I met him at a rest stop in Nebraska and she said "Were you resting?" and she said it sort of sexy and sly and we both smiled and then I told her how he was giving me a ride down to Memphis and she said "Cool."

After Kent came back we watched an episode of The Sopranos for a few minutes and then he said he needed to go spend some time with Albertina's mother and he asked if he could leave us alone together and we both said "Sure" like at almost exactly the same time and then he left.

A few minutes later Albertina said that her

mom liked to see Kent alone and I asked what they did and she said they mostly just talked and that she thought her mom maybe gave him money too and how her stepdad Mark had some bowling league so it was cool and then I asked what her mom did and she said she was a dealer on this big gambling boat called Harrah's and how she got someone to cover her shift so she could hang out with Kent. Then I asked her how long Kent and her mom were married and she said two years which was long enough to have her and then I asked why they broke up and she said she didn't know that he just left one day and then she changed the subject and told me I had a nice face and I said thanks and then we didn't talk for a while.

On TV Tony Soprano was crying in his therapist's office and he seemed way more like a pussy than a mafia boss.

Halfway through the Sopranos Albertina asked me if I wanted to smoke some pot. She said not to worry and that it was legal because her doctor prescribed it.

I said I would totally smoke pot with her so she went into the bathroom and wet a towel with warm water and came back and rolled a joint and we totally got stoned on her medical marijuana and exhaled into the wet towel which is a technique she'd obviously perfected from lots of practice. P it was such good weed it only took me one hit to get high.

Before she took her second hit she told me that she could do the medical brownies thing too but how that gets boring. She said "I prefer rolling doobies." P I think you were the last person I ever heard use the term doobie so that was cool.

We spent about twenty minutes laughing really hard at The Sopranos because it seemed like they were all making these crazy faces like they would only ask you to join the mafia if you could make the same faces.

I totally loved Albertina's laugh. It was like hearing some special breed of bird for the first time. A bird like up in some huge tree in Africa or Paraguay.

After The Sopranos Albertina grabbed the remote and turned the TV off and did this really cool thing which was this she touched my lips. She really touched them P I shit you not and then I touched her lips and she told me my lips were soft and I told her that her lips were softer and we wound up touching each others' lips for like an hour and I am now convinced that lips are the most regal part of the body.

After that we made out and she put my hand down her pants and I felt her for a while and then she put my finger in her and she started rubbing me and things were getting really intense. I couldn't believe how fast it was all happening P but it felt right it really did!

Then I took her PJ Harvey shirt off and her bra too even though it was hard to undo. She totally had to help me I'll admit it and then she took my hoodie off and then my shirt and we were both naked from the waist up and then we just started laughing again.

"I love how white you are!" I heard myself telling her. Man I was high and it was such a beautiful thing P. I mean her breasts were sort of small but they were so PERFECT like they should be put in a museum or something!

Then she told me my nipples were like little stars and we laughed for like ten more minutes.

After our laughter died she asked me if I wanted to do it and that's when I got really quiet. She was like "What?" and then I told her I was a virgin and she said she was too and I said "You are?" and she said "Yeah but what the hell right? I figure I got this stupid disease and my heart sucks and I don't know how much longer I'll be around."

Then I said that was cool but that I didn't have a condom and she said she would call the front desk and that's exactly what she did P I shit you not she called the front desk and said "Can I please have a condom delivered to room 206? . . . Thank you" and a few minutes later this little woman with a green Holiday Inn shirt on knocked on the door and gave us a condom and Albertina tipped her a buck and then we turned the lights out and took our underwear off and sort of eased into the bed like we were easing into warm water and then she put the condom on me and started to feel me more and I told her how I didn't have any pubic hair yet and she was like "Who needs pubic hair?"

My boner was bigger than ever P. I mean I have no idea what it was in terms of inches but in my mind it was huge.

After a minute she lay back and I put it in her really slow at first and then a little faster. Man I was epically excited and I started to even make these noises sort of like baaing or mooing or something. She looked so beautiful with her eyes closed P. She was mad beautiful. I wish I could draw because I would draw it for you.

I really felt like I was making love to her and I

know that's a weird thing to say because of my age but it was really like that for me. She couldn't move around so much and we had to stop a few times so she could get into a more comfortable position because her hips were aching from her lupus but once we got a rhythm going it was like nothing I've ever felt before.

We stayed up all night and I brushed her hair with this special hairbrush she had in her purse and I took some of her hairs when she wasn't looking. They were the ones that came out in the brush and I put them in a piece of Kleenex and then we sort of lay around for a while. I asked her if she wanted to turn the TV back on but she said no that she just wanted to lay there so that's what we did. We just lay there and breathed and sort of looked at each other and sighed.

I said "Albertina" just so I could hear her name out loud and then she said "Punkzilla" and then I told her my real name and she said that too but she told me she liked Punkzilla better. I asked her if I was any good meaning at sex and she said yeah that it was nice and then I asked her if she was bleeding and she said "No I'm fine" which meant that maybe she wasn't a virgin which I have to admit hurt a little but I didn't let it get to me too much. Then Albertina said "Let's hug" which made me feel better so we hugged and fell asleep like that.

I got up in the middle of the night to take a piss and she had put her PJ Harvey T-shirt back on but she was sleeping really deeply like way way down. I wanted to wake her and tell her I loved her but I was afraid P.

When I woke up the next day it was late like eleven-something in the morning and Albertina was gone and there was a note from Kent on the table by the window which said that he had taken Al back to her mother's and that he would see me in a bit.

But Kent never came back P.

I waited like six hours and when I asked about him at the front desk this man with nicotine stains in his mustache said he had paid for the room and left. I asked him if there was a girl with blond hair with him and he said yes and then I asked if she seemed okay and he said that she seemed fine.

I have no idea what happened P. Maybe Kent saw the condom and freaked out or maybe he had always planned to leave me? Maybe Marty was right about that? Maybe he's one of those people who just leaves everyone and maybe I'M one of those people now?

I sat in the motel office and watched the cars coming into the lot and cried. I tried hard to not be a pussy P but I couldn't help it.

Then I tried to call you but it said your phone was disconnected again and that really scares me P. It really scares the shit out of me.

Albertina left her hairbrush behind. It had rolled under the bed. I took her loose hair out of that piece of tissue and put it back in the brush and put the hairbrush inside the Keanu Reeves Halloween mask in the bottom of Sam's backpack. I figure that should protect it pretty good. I wish I could have gotten her phone number or even her e-mail address but I didn't and that sucks.

I wound up getting on another Greyhound P. It was one that left from this part of Joliet called Shorewood. I had to take a cab to the pickup place. Long story short my bus gets into Memphis at seven o'clock tomorrow morning. I guess that's pretty funny right me being on another Greyhound?

Anyway I wanted to let you know that I'm definitely heading south on Interstate 55 and writing this letter has kept my head together.

I know I'm a pretty fucked-up person for saying this P but I hope some bad shit happens to Kent like maybe he'll get his ass kicked or maybe he'll lose his wallet somewhere or maybe he'll have a head-on collision with some semi and his LeBaron will wind up looking like a smashed Coke can.

Anyway I'm finally getting close to Memphis and I'll be fifteen the day after tomorrow and I can't wait to see you.

Love,
Your Bro

March 15, 2008

Dear Albertina,

I have your hairbrush and some of your hair.

I'm on a Greyhound bus heading to Memphis.

I just wanted to tell you I love you.

Someday I will find your address and send this letter to you and your hairbrush too.

Love,
Zilla

March 22, 2008

Dear P,

I got to Memphis 6 days ago.

You are dead and I can't believe how shitty this world is.

I'm sorry P.

I'm so sorry I didn't make it sooner. There are tears all over this notebook but I tried my best I really did.

When the bus got in I took a cab to your address and I knocked on the door and Jorge answered and there were these three hospice nurses and they were gathering in your kitchen and discussing some intense stuff. They were all really nice but I liked the black one Willie best. She had a nice smile and she was pretty and talked to me more than the other two. She told me what was going on with your body and how your liver was failing and how the toxicity in your system was at a peak which meant your other internal organs were going to start failing and how your heart would stop and it was like she was talking about a body not a person or maybe even a car or a washing machine or something but she was mad sensitive about it too. She sat with me at the kitchen table and Jorge was there too.

I was so exhausted I slept through most of my fifteenth birthday not that that even matters at this point.

When I finally woke up I pretty much hung out with you in your hospice room and read you some of these letters I've been writing because Jorge said you could still hear us and that it made you feel loved and I let him listen to them too and he laughed a lot and kept saying I was crazy but in a nice way and sometimes he left me alone with you too.

Your hospice room was really nice P. Jorge put some of his paintings up like the one of the boy in the wolf costume that you loved so much and the one of the diner with the couple kissing and the tornado in the background and he set up all these old photos of you doing your plays and ones of you and him on some road trip you took to Vermont like in little diners and at this weird taco place in Connecticut that's like a haunted house.

And there were copies of your plays on this table near the bed. I had no idea you wrote so many plays P! I counted eighteen of them! Eighteen plays P! You were like Shakespeare! That's so many plays!

Jorge gave me one that wasn't in the pile too. It's called Ice and Water and he said it's about two brothers who go ice fishing on a frozen lake. I can't wait to read that P. I know it will be amazing.

The memorial service was yesterday. It was in this little cemetery in Memphis not far from the Wolf River. Mom and the Major and Edward and Aunt Julie and Grandma Beauty were there but they never saw me. I think Cornelia Zenkich was there too because I think she's dating Edward now but I didn't recognize her. She looked way too clean like she was in a Disney movie or something.

Even though you chose to be cremated Jorge made this little wooden bench for you and everyone gathered around it while Jorge and a few of your friends from your theater group made a circle around the bench and sang some songs and talked about you.

I was really far away like up on this hill and behind a tree with a bunch of birds and tombstones so I couldn't really hear what anyone was saying. The Major was wearing his dress greens and Mom was wearing a black dress with a veil and she was holding flowers and she kept wiping her face with a tissue and E was in a nice suit with a tie and he looked all chiseled like a superhero and Aunt Julie was also wearing a black dress and she was helping Grandma Beauty stand. I think Grandma Beauty was having a hard time with her arthritis or maybe she was just really sad. Jorge was wearing a seersucker suit and a nice old-fashioned hat and he was holding the exact same kind of flowers as Mom and this other guy named Leroy was wearing a black dress too and he was as black as the dress and really tall maybe like six eight or something and mad gay like supergay and you could tell even from the top of the hill and behind that tree where I was hiding that he was making the Major pretty uncomfortable. At one point Leroy went up to him and introduced himself and the Major shook his hand but he was so tense I thought he was going to get stuck like that time his back went out on Christmas Eve and you and Edward had to carry him into his room. The handshake with Leroy was pretty funny P you would have laughed.

I almost came out from behind the tree and walked up to everyone but I couldn't. I guess I just feel outside of their lives now. Like I'm a ghost. Like I need to live everywhere they're NOT. Like I can't ever go back to Cincinnati or my life will get

poisoned and I'll wind up living in the fixed-up basement and I'll start to fade into the new paneling or
something.

But don't worry P because I'm going to stay with
Jorge for a little while and maybe go to school here
in Memphis. I'll probably have to change my name
or get a new identity so I don't come up on some
missing-persons computer.

Jorge says he's going to look out for me. Maybe
I'll just skip school completely and I'll become a
glassblower or I'll learn how to play the guitar and
form that punk band I was telling you about before.

The hospice nurses have been taking all your
medical stuff out of your room and Jorge says that
that's where I can sleep if I want. At first I thought
maybe it would be all weird and haunted but then I
thought that it would be cool if you came and visited
me. I mean it would right? Like every few weeks you
could just appear as a ghost and we could talk or just
hang out and play music for each other.

Anyway I have no idea what I'm going to do with
my life P. I wish we could have talked but when I got
to your apartment you were already unconscious and
man you looked really bad and so skinny like some
other version of you like you became a little old man

and you didn't have any hair and you had all these bruises on your sides and spots on your face and it was really painful to see. I don't think I ever cried so much. I'm going to have to stare at your high school graduation photo that Jorge has hanging in the living room for like a year before I get that other version of you out of my head.

After everyone left the memorial service I came down the hill so I could see the bench and like talk to you a little. The bench has this little brass plate on it with your name and "POET OF THE THEATRE" under it and the dates that you were alive which seems really short for a life P. Twenty-seven years is not that many but Jorge pointed out that that's how old Kurt Cobain was when he died and Janis Joplin and Jimmy Hendrix and this other English songwriter guy Nick Drake who Jorge said you were really getting into before you died. Jorge said he would burn me a CD of his stuff.

I know you'll never get this last letter but maybe you can hear it somehow. Like maybe your soul gets more power after you die or like the words find your ghost or maybe you'll just hang out on the bench every so often which is a nice idea because it's pretty here in this cemetery with all the trees and the tombstones. There is this old man on a riding mower and he just looked over and waved and it's spring so you can smell the grass and the buds in the trees and you can even smell the Wolf River a little. It's getting to that point where you don't have to wear a jacket anymore.

And by the way Jorge said I could use some of your clothes so I'm wearing this old Lou Reed T-shirt of yours right now as I'm writing this on your bench. I'm wearing that with my hoodie and a new pair of New Balances that Jorge bought me the other day. The T-shirt's big on me but I'll grow into it at some point.

So that's all for now P. Maybe I'll write you again when I figure out what I'm going to do. I'll be staying in your room and feeding Carlos the Cat and keeping his litter box clean and I might go back on my medication because Jorge thinks it will help me focus while I figure out what's next.

I might also try and get in touch with Albertina at some point but in some ways that whole experience feels sort of like a dream like one of those perfect dreams that could never be experienced in real life so I'm not sure I want to mess with it.

I'm so sorry you got sick P. You didn't deserve

it. Jorge says you were so brave and I need some of that kind of courage I really do but I'll get there someday.

Love,
Your Bro

December 2, 2007

Dear P,

Hey big bro. You're probably surprised and shit to hear from me huh? I'm worried that you won't ever get this letter because maybe you moved somewhere else like away from Memphis like maybe you're in Athens Georgia with that theater company who paid you to write that play about those nuns who got raped or maybe you're in Puerto Rico with Jorge's family.

I wanted to let you know that since the last time we spoke on the phone I went AWOL and I mean AWOL as in permanently. Buckner Military Academy has seen the last of me. The Buckner Bison can kiss my skinny ass good-bye.

I'm not going to tell you where I am because I don't want anyone to know especially Mom and the Major and Edward too. Not that you would nark on me. I just don't want there to be any evidence.

Here's a hint. You could call it P-town but nobody actually calls it that. Here's another hint and it's a harder one because you don't know anything about sports. It's where the Trail Blazers play. The Trail Blazers are a basketball team and they've been really bad for a long time but they're starting to be pretty good again and everyone here wears Trail Blazers puffy coats and baseball hats and it's like a religion here.

Anyway I just wanted to say hi and let you know that I'm okay even though I ran out of my medication and that's starting to make me tense. There's this kid I met who has ADD too but he doesn't take Ritalin he takes this other stuff called Dexadrim so I might be able to use his stuff for a little while.

How are things with you? How's Jorge? Is he still painting murals? Is he still shaving his head? How are your performance pieces going? Aren't they called monologues? Is that a play too? Or a drama or whatever?

Just so you know I'm not in school right now which is fun. I realize I am digging my own grave by not taking my medication and being a truant (that's the official word right?) but I'm learning a lot about the world and about life in general. And I'm meeting chicks which wasn't happening at all at Buckner. I'm mostly hanging out at night and making some money and trying to stay out of trouble meaning away from the cops.

Shit! I just realized that you can't write back to

me unless I tell you where I am. Okay so P-town is Portland Oregon NOT PORTLAND MAINE and I'll write the address on the back of the envelope but don't show anyone this letter. You should maybe burn it after you copy the address down. Seriously burn it P.

Sometimes I'm so fucking stupid.

Hope you have a nice Christmas with Jorge. Did you get a tree? Do you guys still have Carlos?

Love,
Your Bro

A stolen car. A kidnapped baby.

And three teenagers with pasts they can't outrun.

33 Snowfish
by Adam Rapp

"Ferocious . . . lunatic . . . absolutely brilliant."
— M. T. Anderson, author of *Feed*

"Custis is a weedy preteen who's been unwanted and abused, Curl is a teenage prostitute trying not to slip back into a drug habit, and Boobie, the light of their lives, is a quiet, magnetic, and disturbed young man. . . . A book rare in its brutally frank treatment of the unresolved tragedy that is many young people's lives."
— *Bulletin of the Center for Children's Books*

www.candlewick.com

Sometimes you have to look at who you were to know who you are.

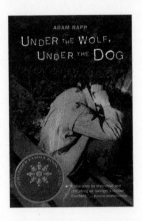

Under the Wolf, Under the Dog
by Adam Rapp

A *Los Angeles Times* Book Prize Finalist

A Schneider Family Book Award Winner

★ "Steve Nugent is a character as distinctive and disturbing as Salinger's Holden Caulfield was 50 years ago. . . . Teens will root from their hearts and even laugh a little as Steve struggles to fight his way out from under the dog of depression that has him pinned down." — *Booklist* (starred review)